A young master of contemporary political history, from Finland, with a life-long passion in literature, Europaeus wants to fuse his interests and skills to shine light on some of the recent centuries' lesser-known but equally important events through his writing. Besides his studies in Finland and work in literature, Europaeus has studied in The Netherlands, interned at the Embassy of Finland in Türkiye, and worked for Accenture, in Ireland.

To my parents, who always believed in my work.

Otto Europaeus

CLIPPED WINGS

AUSTIN MACAULEY PUBLISHERS™
LONDON • CAMBRIDGE • NEW YORK • SHARJAH

Copyright © Otto Europaeus 2023

The right of Otto Europaeus to be identified as author of this work has been asserted by the author in accordance with sections 77 and 78 of the Copyright, Designs and Patents Act 1988.

All rights reserved. No part of this publication may be reproduced, stored in a retrieval system, or transmitted in any form or by any means, electronic, mechanical, photocopying, recording, or otherwise, without the prior permission of the publishers.

Any person who commits any unauthorized act in relation to this publication may be liable to criminal prosecution and civil claims for damages.

This is a work of fiction. Names, characters, businesses, places, events, locales, and incidents are either the products of the author's imagination or used in a fictitious manner. Any resemblance to actual persons, living or dead, or actual events is purely coincidental.

A CIP catalogue record for this title is available from the British Library.

ISBN 9781035818648 (Paperback)
ISBN 9781035818655 (ePub e-book)

www.austinmacauley.com

First Published 2023
Austin Macauley Publishers Ltd®
1 Canada Square
Canary Wharf
London
E14 5AA

Table of Contents

1. Butterfly	9
2. Certain Gentleman	15
3. Punished	37
4. Heavier Hand	57
5. Father	66
6. Thousand Sheets	74
7. The Blind and the Timid	95
8. The Estranged	112
9. Minor Noble's Grand Adventure	122
10. Faithful	143
11. Pet Monkey	150
12. The Unwanted	164
13. Clipped Wings	184

1. Butterfly

The late evening was like any other in the past years. The sun was setting behind the tree line in the distance, marking the end of a day's labour and the last drops of rubber to be drawn until the sun rose again. It was the mark Nsala had been waiting for: the mark to pick up his half-empty bucket and knife, and head home. Or at least to the closest thing he had for one.

It was a long walk there. He met others along the way, all with similar tools in tow. They shared a narrow trail together, but didn't speak. No one really had anything to say, and even if they did, none had the spare energy to share their thoughts aloud. By the time they arrived home, little daylight remained.

The night, too, would've been like any other in the past years, but on this particular one, something had stirred the exhausted workers out of their huts. It was something important enough for them to lose some of their short rest for. A crowd had already gathered in the small town's centre, in a half-circle. They had their back turned on the late stragglers who only now arrived on the scene.

Someone turned around and noted one of the approaching men.

"Nsala, stop," a voice said, before a hand pressed against his chest. "You don't want to go any further."

"What? What's going on?"

"You don't need to see this."

"See what?" Nsala asked.

He dropped the bucket and knife. He shoved the hand aside and stood up on his toes to reach over the restless crowd. In the middle of it, he caught a glimpse of people sitting on their knees, surrounded by soldiers donning the foreigners' blue uniforms and red caps.

"Nsala, please. You don't need to see this," a voice said before another hand tried to take hold of his shoulder.

He shook it off and pushed the people in front of him away. He made his way through the crowd without much resistance while whispers began to fill the air. Eyes turned to him. Some turned downwards to the wet mud, some widened, and others ignored him, until there were no more people to push through, and he stood in the front alone.

He saw two men, a woman and a girl sitting on thin, soaked carpets, their hands and legs tied. All looked down, too tired or afraid to look anywhere else.

He didn't want to believe what his eyes told him. The girl, she looked familiar, but from this distance and without being able to see her face clearly, he wasn't sure. He didn't want to be sure. Maybe the voices in the crowd had been correct. Maybe he should just look away.

The girl raised her head. She noticed a familiar face in the seething mass. "Father!"

"Oleka?" Nsala shouted back. "…what's going on? Is that you?"

The words had barely passed from his lips when he took a sharp step forward. He didn't think about it at all. Another followed, and the walk turned into a dash. A dash that was stopped before it even began, by three rifles raised directly at him. One of the carriers, a man like him, shouted in a foreign tongue.

Nsala stopped. He hesitated. He breathed in the wet air. A slight tremble ran across his body as he looked at one of the men. Their eyes met past the rifle's iron sights.

A voice urged him to step back. His voice or someone else's? Another voice, this one much clearer, urged him forward. He listened to the latter and took a step forward.

The soldier repeated what he had just said, but when that didn't stop the lone man from approaching, another shouted a more understandable word.

"Stop!"

Nsala turned his head towards the shout's direction. He didn't see the rifle stock that hit his chest. It knocked all air out of his lungs. A girl's scream rang in the air before it got muffled by piles of mud burrowing inside his ears.

Hands grasped his legs. They were ones that he couldn't shake off. The image of the girl became blurry and distant to him. Then a foot pressed down on his back, leaving him unable to even move his head. All he could do was squint his eyes to try and see better.

He saw a soldier, larger than the others. One that walked in front of the four prisoners like nothing had just happened. The brute stepped forward slowly, taking his time, before bracing his bare feet deep into the soft ground. Then he waited, waited for the little girl's cry to die down, and then waited some more.

"These people," he bellowed all of a sudden, "have been brought before you all. For the sake of brevity, know only that the two men, the woman's husband, and the girl's father have all been found guilty of shirking their duties to the crown. They have failed to provide the expected amount of rubber demanded of them for every two weeks. It stands to reason then that either the accused or their close relatives should be punished for their laziness and reluctance to contribute towards the common good of the Free State."

With each passing word, the lone brute's chest bulged and contracted. He emphasized every word and spoke without a flaw in the foreigners' tongue. And the more he shouted, the more animated the crowd became as it picked up individual words here and there. Initial murmur turned into dissenting voices and then erupted into a cacophony of pleads.

"No, you can't do this to them!"

"Have mercy on them!"

"They don't deserve this, none of them do!"

"Silence!" the brute's voice pierced the air, and the crowd obeyed. He picked up from where he had left off, "The punishment for such insolence is clear: one hand of each offender or that of their close relative will be cut off so that the offenders, and those around them, will better remember the consequences that their shirking of duty has brought."

Voices from the crowd erupted again. This time the brute ignored them and shouted over them, "Following that, the two men and the woman will be taken elsewhere to provide labour for the Free State. The girl, on the other hand, is not fit for this purpose, and will be released back to her family."

Nsala still struggled to catch his breath. His head was sideways in the mud, his eyes locked with the girl's. She was quiet now. Either she didn't understand what was going on, the gravity of the brute's words, or she had already screamed her lungs dry.

A shot rang in the air to quell the crowd for one final time. A stillness descended over the night. No one said a word when the brute placed a wooden block in front of the first victim. No one hushed when he untied the robes around his wrists and placed his hand over the chopping block and held it there, like a butcher preparing to chop a piece of meat. No one breathed when he brought the forward-leaning blade down on the wrist, ignored the scream and jerked the blade free, only to repeat the action. He tossed the bloodied stump to a bag held by another soldier. Then he prepared to do the same again.

"Please, kind sir…don't do this," Nsala sobbed. "Don't do this."

A small, cold metal cylinder pressed itself against his neck. Nsala closed his eyes, fell quiet and swallowed hard, before uttering again, "Please, take my hand instead."

His plea fell on empty ears. The brute severed the other man's hand. He was silent as a grave.

"Don't do this, kind sir. Take my hand instead," Nsala begged, this time in the foreigners' language. The only thing it achieved was that the metal cylinder pressed itself tighter against his neck.

The woman was next. Just before the brute got to her, she tried to spring up, but only managed to fall on her side next to the girl who joined in with the scream. Two soldiers picked up the woman and held her there while the brute measured her hand over the chopping block. She fainted. Before or after the deed, that was impossible to tell, whether she felt pain or not.

There was only one more victim left. One more hand, and they could all go home and to sleep. The brute took hold of the girl's little hand.

"Father! Do something."

"Please, take my hand instead, kind sir. Take my hand instead."

A face in the background turned to him. A face different from all the others. "Don't let them!" the girl screamed. "Stop them…"

"Take my hand instead, kind sir. Take both of them."

"Why aren't you…?"

Rain. It rained often in Northern Congo in April. The rainy season has just begun a couple of weeks ago. The water felt warm.

2. Certain Gentleman

Most of the time the air stood still over Lake Mantumba. Sometimes a fish might leap from the water in pursuit of some insect, or a hippopotamus surfaced to yawn before sinking back to the bottom. Now the only sound breaking the silence was that of an occasional pebble being tossed into the water. Some of them skipped once or twice before drifting under the surface, while others plummeted straight down.

Even the water's presence couldn't ease the heat in the air. It was the kind of oppressing heat where raising one's sleeves by an inch brought about a cooling bliss for a few seconds. Something that would also inevitably attract the buzzing mosquitoes in the thick air. One of them followed the scent of sweat to a warm, soft surface, just before a descending shadow crushed it.

"How can anyone stand for these little fuckers?" A young man yelled. He lifted his hand and looked at the bloody smear that remained, "Look, it's already bitten someone."

"Don't roll up your sleeves then," a man next to him said.

"If I don't, then I'd just be swimming in my own sweat."

"You get accustomed to it over time, Henrik, but to malaria, not so much."

"That's easy for you to say. You can't get it," Henrik said and lifted his narrowed eyes towards the black man. "Why would anyone want to come to this God forsaken sorry backwater?"

"You should know the answer to that yourself. You're the one who chose to leave Europe behind and come here."

Henrik didn't have an answer at hand. He contented himself with a grunt, and then muttered, "Congo isn't what I thought it'd be."

"And what did you expect? That you could cruise around the river in the latest steamship, shoot anybody who looked at you the wrong way without fear of consequence, and search the jungles for some lost treasure. That's the reason you came here, isn't it? None of that cumbersome European decency to weigh you down."

"Oh, fuck off, David. The only reason you're sitting here with me and not working your ass off in the plantations is because your own parents let the Belgians take you with them."

This time it was David's turn to fall silent. He looked out in the distance, and then picked up another stone without a word. It too sunk beneath the water, followed by a second. The uneasy silence lasted until a soft buzzing noise approached an open arm. It was followed by another smack and a litany of swear words.

"Can you already feel the white man's burden weighing down your back?" David chuckled. "Keep laughing, and it's going to be you who gets to go hunting hippos next week."

Just then their attention turned elsewhere. A narrow trail of rising smoke appeared behind a cape covered in vegetation. It announced the arrival of a small steamboat minutes before it could be seen. It wasn't one of the rare cargo boats, or even rarer passenger ships that arrived at scheduled intervals, but a completely unexpected arrival. And at the boat's helm stood a tall, lone man looking like he was coming to visit the finest café in Paris for a glass of afternoon champagne.

"Now who the hell is that?"

"I've no idea," Henrik said and stood up. "Should we let him dock?"

"Of course. He's white, like you. I don't know who he is, but he must be someone important to come all the way here."

"Alright, let's see just who our unexpected guest is," Henrik said. He stood up and beckoned at the man in the distance.

The tall man nodded, and slipped under a makeshift roof. Soon the boat came to a halt sideways to the pier, and the man got off with a stumble before the boat had been tied up properly. A large bulldog followed him out of the boat.

Upon closer inspection, it became evident that the man had already spent his own fair share of time in Congo instead of having left Le Havre two months ago. Light-yellow stains marked the armpits of his white, tall-collared shirt. His black, curly hair and swirly beard hadn't been properly trimmed in some time, his cheeks were sunken, and his skin had taken a brown tint to it. Some old scratches marked his hands. The somewhat ghoulish frame surrounded a pair of keen, deep-blue eyes that stood in stark contrast to everything else.

The young man hesitated for a moment before uttering in French, "Welcome to Bikoro. I'm Henrik Mikael af Älvängen, and I'm the subordinate official here."

"Swedish, I presume?" the tall man asked and presented an open hand.

The youngster gave a flimsy handshake before adding, "Yeah, from around Gothenburg."

"And of nobility?"

"Minor only."

"Congo draws all kinds of mismatches to it, doesn't it?"

"Seems like so. And you are?"

"Sir Roger Casement, His Majesty Edward the Seventh's, King of Great Britain's, consul to the Congo Free State," the tall man presented himself with a low, dull voice that lacked any fanfare. "I work for the foreign office, and I've been sent here to prepare a report on the Free State's general condition. As such, I'd like to meet whoever is in charge of this trading outpost."

Henrik looked like he barely comprehended the meaning of the stranger's words. Then he glanced at the black soldier next to him, darted his eyes down and scratched his bare chin.

"You said you were the subordinate official, didn't you, young chap?"

"Yeah, I did."

"Then I believe it should be up to you to introduce me to whoever's in charge."

"Fine, wait here," Henrik groaned before bringing his eyes back to the black soldier. "David, stay with him. I'll be back soon."

"As you wish, sir," David said with a nod.

The young officer left. David offered his help to secure the steamboat to the pier, and just when that was done, Henrik returned skulking behind someone who kept a brisk pace.

"A new face, all the way over here!" the man announced. "You must be none other than that new clerk I've been waiting for months."

"I am not, unfortunately," Roger answered and proceeded to introduce himself a second time.

"An Englishman all the way over here?"

"An Irishman, to be exact."

"A subject of the British Crown all the same."

"Well yes, and with whom do I have the pleasure to speak with?"

"Gaspard Bunschoten, Chief of the Post here in Bikoro, and the Executive Chief of the Mantumba district," the man presented himself and gave the extended hand a firm shake. "At least, that's the whole job title. In short, I'm responsible for making sure that everything around here runs smoothly."

Under the title Gaspard appeared rather unremarkable. The only defining feature on him was a finely-brushed moustache that peeked under the cap of his white helmet. The other saving aspect from ordinary was his immaculate sense of fashion that consisted of a snowy jacket, grey trousers, silk necktie and tall, varnished boots. He didn't have a single drop of sweat on his clothes or on his bronzed skin.

"Bikoro is property of the Free State, is that correct?"

Roger continued. "It is."

"Then do you already know the reason for my presence here?"

"I don't. News travel slowly around here, but it must be something important, I'd wager, for a foreign consul to show up here. We rarely get visitors."

"You're correct about that. I won't mince my words, Mr Bunschoten, and will go straight to business," Roger said without a change in his tone. "A few months ago, I received a telegram from London that instructed me to look into the alleged abuse of the local populace at the Free State's hands. Abuse that has been going on for some thirteen years, and has been backed by numerous witnesses representing…"

"So very British of you, I think."

"Excuse me?"

"How you skipped straight to the point without the formalities," Gaspard said. "You see, before we proceed on this matter and discuss state affairs, I'd like to see proof that you truly are who you claim to be. Formalities on behalf of the Free State, I'm afraid. I'm sure you understand, as a consul."

"Of course, excuse me. Spend enough time alone and you begin to forget the niceties of formal conversations," Roger said.

He reached inside a pocket in his loose black pants, and presented two papers.

"The first one is a document proving my identity, and the second is a letter from the local authority at Leopoldville giving their blessing to my investigation."

"May I see them?" Gaspard asked, and Roger obliged. Gaspard skimmed through both of them before commenting, "They seem genuine, and so does your reason for being here. You must however excuse me, Mr Casement, it's just that I'm somewhat…"

"Confused?"

"Surprised, by your arrival," Gaspard corrected as Roger clicked his tongue. "Furthermore, the letter approving of your travel upstream was signed almost a month ago, while I haven't received anything from anyone informing of your arrival, even if there's only a day's journey by boat to the closest telegraph station."

"At first, I planned to board a state-owned steamer, but as it was already full, American missionaries offered me passage on their steamer. They then refused to progress past their station, so I ended up renting my own riverboat."

"I see. That explains a lot. That, and the fact that the postal service isn't exactly reliable this deep in the African interior," Gaspard spoke more to himself. "Furthermore, I wouldn't expect anyone to crawl this far inland unless they were paid to do so. That's the reason why I'm here, after all, and not in Brussels. So, Mr Casement, I bid you welcome. If nothing else, your unexpected visit offers a much-needed change of pace to the tedious routine around here."

"Not much going on, then?"

Gaspard gave his words a tired laugh, "Nothing at all. Your arrival is the single most exciting thing that has happened here all summer. I'm actually glad you weren't the new clerk."

"How come?"

"I started bookkeeping on my own accord after my old clerk died of malaria back in early February, I think. Or perhaps it was late January. Time runs so slowly here that sometimes it feels like a loop, where every day repeats the one before it," Gaspard mulled. "Anyway, Henrik has been of help, to a degree, but I still do most of the bookkeeping as it gives me something to do."

"I must agree with you. I've spent the last three years listening to complaints of drunken sailors and arranging tickets for impoverished young men to get home."

"Ha, but you must know of all the latest developments in Europe," Gaspard said and hovered his hand over Roger's back. "Come on inside then. We have a lot to talk about these allegations and the British crown's interest in them."

"May John join us?"

"Your dog? Of course. I have no problem with that."

"May I join as well?" Henrik asked.

Gaspard barely stopped before dismissing him, "No, boy. This is important business, and above what you're paid."

The dog traipsed past the disappointed officer who was left on the docks.

Some logs were stored next to the pier, meant as fuel for the rare passing steamer. Few stubby palm trees stood by the shore and did their best to hide a white manor built to emulate houses that one would find more readily in the European countryside.

A small, open courtyard was situated next to the manor. Opposite to it were two small guesthouses, and next to them was a small vegetable garden and a pen for a handful of short-haired sheep. In the middle of the courtyard stood a flagpole. Against it flopped a dark blue bundle that hid in its seams a golden star that should've represented the light of civilization in a dark night.

Gaspard led Roger inside the manor and past mosquito nets to an open living room. The room was built entirely out of smooth planks painted in white, and the open door and windows let in golden afternoon light that gave the space a peaceful atmosphere. In the middle of it stood a wide table and three wicker chairs covered in red pillows. Plant pots lined the walls.

On one side table was an ivory statuette. It stood there as a reminder of the land's former riches from a not-so-distant past. Nowadays no one cared about ivory anymore, and the only thing anyone in Congo listened to was the constant demand for wild India-rubber to flow back to the civilized world. As if to ensure that those demands were met, a silver lined portrait of the Belgian King, Leopold the Second, hung over the statuette to remind all that this land, and everything on it, was his personal property. Yet not even the artist's brush had been able to shake off the king's awkward backward-leaning posture, sour eyes and grey beard that dominated the picture.

"You have his majesty's portrait on your wall," Roger commented.

"I do. It was a gift from him," Gaspard said and stoked the pillows on one chair. "Every official receives one such portrait before leaving Belgium to Congo."

"Yes, I know. I met him in Brussels as well before coming here. He wasn't exactly a likeable person."

"No, he isn't, to be honest. A prudent monarch to be sure, and one that shows genuine concern for his subjects' wellbeing, but not an especially pleasant person to be around. I, however, think that makes him all the more qualified for the role."

"How come? When I think of a monarch, the first image that comes to my mind is a public speaker, able to rally thousands with a few words."

"That depends on how you measure a monarch's merit. If you do it by the vastness of their lands, well, the emperor of Russia comes first. If by the might of their military, the

German emperor, of course. And if by the length of their rule, the late Victoria has no equal."

"Bless her memory."

Gaspard nodded before continuing, "But if we measure a monarch's merit by their wisdom, Leopold would be a prime candidate as the greatest monarch alive. Belgium may be a small country with small people, as he famously said, but he's a philosopher king, as described by Plato, and fully dedicated to improving the wellbeing of his subjects both back home and abroad."

"You're a well-read man, I take?"

"Somewhat. Being stuck here has left me with a lot of time for that, in the vein of my king."

"I can admire that," Roger said and finally sat down as well, opposite of his host. "But under his majesty's august eyes, perhaps we should turn to my reason for being here."

"Of course. Please, speak your mind."

"Well, as I already told by the pier, the British government requested me to look into the alleged reports of human right abuses that have made headlines in the European and North-American media in the recent thirteen years, but especially in the past two years."

"Yes, horrible accusations. Horrible indeed." Gaspard muttered. "I have heard of these sad news as well, but they always begin with 'it's alleged, it's reported', and so on."

"Indeed. I've learned that people tend to speak much, but I'm interested in more than just words."

"Then I hope I can help clear any and all doubts you might harbour over them."

Roger crossed his right leg over his left leg and continued, "With these accusations, I'm more closely referring to the ones by the British journalist, Edmund Morel, whose stream of articles and leaked information about the Free State has caused quite a commotion back home in Britain."

"I know him. I've never met him, of course, but he hardly seems to sleep. There's a steamer that brings post here every three weeks, and Morel's writings are a staple among them. That has made him a constant thorn sticking to Leopold's side."

"Yes, and he has gathered quite a following with his writings. For example, Morel has claimed that since the Belgian imports to Congo consist of little more than weapons and ammunition, and with consideration given to the colony's sizeable surface area, it stands to reason that the immense exports of India-rubber and agricultural products are only possible by forced labour," Roger told. "I'm no economist, Mr Bunschoten, but it doesn't take one to realize how all other alternatives of production seem improbable."

"And such claims are what your government sent you here to investigate?"

"They are. And I'm interested to know what you make out of them."

"To my knowing, Morel has never been to Congo, whereas I've given almost ten years of my life to Congo."

"Admirable. I, in turn, have spent close to twenty years in Africa, half of my entire life."

"Is that so?" Gaspard asked and leaned in closer, hands on his knees. "Then we two veterans have more first-hand knowledge of Congo than most others, and shouldn't have to rely on such second-hand sources."

"As much as I hate to admit it, however, I haven't been this far from Leopoldville in sixteen years. And I've worked in several other Britain's African colonies as well, so I can't speak for the current situation here in Upper Congo."

"I see. Do you usually work in Boma?"

"Yes."

"Say, then, what's your opinion of the capital."

"It's a charming little place with the makings of a proper city one day. I was actually there when the town was established, and worked on the railroad that connects the coast to Leopoldville."

"Is that so?"

"Yes, although that was years before the actual construction work began. I was a naïve idealist from Europe assisting the land surveyors in planning the route around the rapids that make boat travel impossible. Now that I think of it, I resembled the young Henrik. And just like him, I came to be disappointed with what I saw in Congo."

"But you still chose to stay."

"I did."

"Why exactly?"

"You either accept the dull reality that Africa has to offer, that it's not the final frontier, full of adventure and wealth that everyone makes it out to be, or you go back home and accept the dull reality of your old life that at least has some comfort to it in the way of familiarity. The only difference is that outside of the overpopulated Europe you can still be someone."

"I must agree with you completely. I would've been nothing in Belgium, but here I can be that someone."

"Yes, which brings us right back here, to this present moment."

Gaspard leaned back and muttered. "Of course. Has your work then given any confirmation to these rumours?"

"So far I have verified only two cases of uncalled violence and cruelty. The first one happened towards the end of the year 1900, and involved a white officer who led an armed expedition through some dozen villages. He ended up looting, burning and killing his way across the countryside until he satisfied whatever motive set him on that path."

"That one? Yes, I remember as well. The young rascal was punished for his 'adventures' by the government and forced to pay reparations to the victims' loved ones. That self-righteous crusade bankrupted him for life!" Gaspard answered.

Roger gave him a nod, and Gaspard asked, "What about the other one?"

"The second case happened in the summer of that same year, and involved a certain British citizen and three other Europeans. They had taken local women and children as hostages, to force their husbands and fathers to collect India-rubber from the jungles."

"I've heard of that one as well. Around a hundred or so natives died at their hands."

"Indeed, but in the end justice was done again. I met the British subject in early 1901. He pleaded for his innocence, but no amount of tears could earn him my remorse, or save him from the long prison sentence waiting for him."

"Very good, I would've done the exact same in your boots," Gaspard said. "So then, if these two cases are the only ones you have heard of, and they both ended with the guilty being punished as they should, why have you come all this way?"

"Because they are the only two confirmed cases. As I said, I haven't visited Upper Congo in sixteen years, and the amount of rumours floating downstream to Europe has been much more than that."

"I understand that, but have you seen or heard anything similar to these two cases?"

"Not yet, something that I'm thankful for. There's however one case that I've witnessed with my own eyes, although it happened a long time ago," Roger mentioned. "A white officer and his black subordinates were abusing a local boy. I stepped in and saved the boy's life, but in the end nothing happened to the officer."

"Why is that?"

"The judge ruled that the scars on the boy's back from the officer's whip weren't enough proof that he had been abused."

"Correct."

"You agree with the judge?"

"I do," Gaspard said with a nod. "Although I'd like to believe you are right, from what I understood, your words were the only proof that the scars were given by the officer. One man's word is not enough."

"There were the soldiers as well, but they refused to speak on the matter. And so did the boy."

"In the other two cases you described there were more witnesses, and the victims were ready to testify. This incident with the boy happened, what, sixteen years ago?" Gaspard asked. "A lot has changed since then."

"Hopefully. But at the same time I know what I saw back then was wrong," Roger said. "If nothing else, that case and my memory of Upper Congo provide useful points of reference in measuring how things have changed in the past decade and a half."

"Have they changed for better or worse?"

"Mostly for the worse. Today's Congo appears a much more...desolate place," Roger told. "Almost all of the locals that I've met were in a sad state, and complained about hard labour and lack of food. I also met a large group of locals who had fled on foot a government-imposed rubber tax, and left behind almost all of their possessions. When I asked their reason for doing so, they told that they hadn't received payment for their work, had faced starvation, and suffered from a lack of firewood to warm themselves at night. And when the India-rubber had grown rare, soldiers mutilated some men's private parts or outright shot them," Roger told before pausing for a moment. "Sometimes, it was the government official who performed the deeds."

"That certainly wasn't me," Gaspard almost shouted.

"I'm not claiming that," Roger hurried to add. "Moreover, I wasn't able to prove the veracity of their statements, and to be honest, some of them sounded exaggerated or outright invented. It's imperative to my work that I maintain an impartial look on everything."

"That is a good principle to follow. I imagine your superiors back home want an accurate report instead of another scoop meant to infuriate readers."

"However, we cannot just dismiss the claims either."

"No, but the two juridical cases you brought up should give you plenty of evidence that the Free State has improved in this regard from the days you were working on the railroad. Sixteen years is a long time to make a lot of good progress. Nowadays the state keeps track of such cases and reprimands the ones responsible for going against the king's humanitarian goals."

"It's reassuring, I admit, but the way these people spoke of their experiences, with open eyes and shaking voices, gave their words conviction. Not to mention that the stories matched one another. Claims like that are what I'm looking for here."

"Mr Casement, let me assure you, if there's anything that I can do to help you with your work, and to quell your doubts, I will do it. And I sincerely hope that you won't find anything more than stories here."

Roger contented himself with a hum. His eyes moved down to the floor, at the bulldog that had crawled to sleep at his feet.

"How about we drink to that, Mr Casement?" Gaspard asked and leaned forward. "I have some bottles of vintage wine that I've been saving."

"It's not really my thing, but I guess I can drink a little."

"Wonderful," Gaspard nodded and turned towards an open doorway. "Julienne, be a dear and bring a bottle of Château Latour with two glasses."

"Julienne…is she your wife?"

"Goodness, no," Gaspard dismissed with a shy laugh. "She's the household servant."

Roger thought on the words for a moment and then asked, "When she brings in the wine, do you mind if I ask her a couple of questions."

"Not at all."

Soon a young, short woman appeared by the door. She had dark-brown skin and a tall hairline, but unlike so many others Roger had seen, she was dressed in a simple white dress that had seen its fair share of use and was made in cheap imitation of European clothing.

She balanced a wooden tray over her hands with Gaspard's order on it, and placed it carefully on the table with a curtsey. Just when she was about to turn and slip away, Gaspard asked her to stay, and motioned at the guest sitting across the table.

"Before you go, dear, my guest has something to ask from you."

"Yes," Roger said. "Julienne, that is your name, is it not?"

"It is, sir," she said with her eyes turned to the floor.

"Were you born with that name?"

"No sir."

"Who gave it to you?"

"A man, like you. He speaks of god and teaches your language."

"That's good to know," Roger said. "And how are you feeling?"

"I'm good, sir. How are you?"

"I'm feeling good as well," Roger answered with his usual dull voice. "Thank you. I have no more questions right now."

She glanced over her shoulder at Gaspard who shooed her away, "You can go now."

He waited for the servant to disappear behind the doorway. Then he said, "Julienne is shy, and doesn't speak French that much."

"I noticed."

"She is still much better at the language than many others. David, the soldier you met back by the pier, on the other hand, is a model student," Gaspard told and reached for the corkscrew. "He's fluent in the language."

"That's good to know. We hardly spoke a word."

"Then I believe you'd like to speak with him later on."

Gaspard drew the cork with a pop and poured some of the bottle's contents into two wide glasses. He then offered the other glass to Roger and wished him good health.

Roger took the glass and looked at the bottom. He spun the glass around a bit. The liquid followed as a short-lived, transparent vortex before coming to a halt. Then they toasted.

Gaspard felled the entire glass in one sweep, and then asked Roger to follow him outside. Roger stayed behind for a moment. He pressed the glass against his lips, but then hesitated and put the glass back on the table, its contents full, before following Gaspard outside. The bulldog at his feet took a moment to wake up and follow.

"I think we started on a wrong foot," Gaspard said the moment Roger pulled back the mosquito nets. He leaned in against a wooden rail and motioned towards the distance, at straw-roofed huts surrounding the mansion and rows of bushes and trees that grew behind them. He asked, "Is there something I could do for you? What kind of material are you looking for your report?"

"I'd need written materials like documents, letters and ledgers, and if possible, reliable accounts by locals of their daily lives."

"You're free to look into my ledgers, but those are the only documents I can offer. What few letters I have are all personal and confidential."

"I'm not here to inquire into your personal life. The ledgers, however, should help and are much appreciated."

"I'll ask Julienne to procure them for you."

"Thank you."

"As for the natives and their accounts, you can walk around and interview whoever you want. Just be aware of the language barrier. As mentioned, most of the natives are still struggling to grasp the basics of French. And if somebody asks who you are, just say that you have my permission to be here and do your work."

"That will be a tremendous help, thank you. I'm already thinking of touring the plantations tomorrow. Would you like to accompany me and offer your insight?"

"To go and speak with my workers?" Gaspard asked and stood up. Roger nodded, but Gaspard shook his head and refused, "Most don't really like to see me around."

"Why is that?"

"Mr Casement, there is something I meant to tell you earlier, something that you might not like to hear."

"It's alright. I'm not here to judge, only to listen."

Gaspard nodded at the trees in the distance. He cleared his throat and spoke, "The rumours and stories that you came here to investigate, the abuses, kidnappings and killings, they did happen years ago. And it wasn't just about the boy you met or the handful of individuals you've heard about."

"What do you mean?"

"Bikoro used to be one of the main stages for the so-called 'rubber terror'. The Free State official residing here, my predecessor, was especially cruel towards the natives, and mostly resorted to armed violence to keep up the India-rubber collection."

"Do you think he could've been the official the people I spoke with mentioned?"

"That's likely. The terror ended five years ago with reforms made by the government. There weren't many of such cases, but enough to sound the alarm, and to understand what they meant for Leopold's vision," Gaspard said. "For example, when I began here, there were 68 soldiers. Now, only 19. I think it's a step in the right direction."

"And what are the remaining soldiers for?"

"To protect the natives from wild predators, such as leopards, and of course to keep up law in case there's need for it. Furthermore, as the India-rubber harvests around the lake were unprofitable compared to many other areas, Bikoro was transformed into a coffee and cacao plantation, as you can see from all the plantations around us."

"So you don't actually produce any rubber here anymore?"

"Not the wild India-rubber, no, but two years ago we planted a patch of cultivated rubber trees to keep up with the increased demand back home," Gaspard told. He fell quiet, leaned back in and muttered in a silent voice to the ground, "Many of the natives had an awful past at the hands of the previous official, and all of it because of India-rubber. It will take time, years still I'm afraid, for the bond of trust to be restored."

"When I've heard of the many disturbing claims about the treatment of locals, two things have often stood out from the others. The use of leather whips against the natives, and the extensive mutilation of their hands," Roger brought up. "I know the first to be true, because I've witnessed before, but is it still going on?"

"Not in my time in charge of this district."

"And what of the mutilated hands then? Has it taken place at all?"

Gaspard swallowed hard before admitting that it had, "Most of the hands were taken by soldiers during punitive expeditions against villagers who hadn't gathered enough India-rubber, in the past. When the first deeds were exposed, the Free State was quick to bring a stop to them."

"So both have taken place. I appreciate your honesty in this matter," Roger thanked. "It can't be an easy thing to bring up, or talk about. But it begets an important question: are these atrocities still happening elsewhere in the country?"

"I have never done anything like that, but at the same time I can't speak for the whole country. Congo is a vast place, some eighty times the size of Belgium, and moving from one place to another takes considerable time that neither I nor the natives simply have."

After those words, they both fell silent for a moment. Roger leaned in against the wooden rail as well before asking, "The woman, Julienne, your housemaid, mentioned a Christian missionary. Perhaps he would have connections to other missionaries around the country."

"Only to the Roman Catholic ones."

"Nevertheless, I'd like to meet him."

"That can be arranged. Most of the native workers live in a town called Bomenga, some three kilometres to the north from here. The Father lives with them, and teaches them Christian ethics and French. If you still intend to do that tour of yours tomorrow, you should pay him a visit there."

"That sounds good. In the meanwhile, I'd like to spend the rest of the evening going through those ledgers you mentioned."

"Of course. And while you do that, I'll tell Henrik and David to prepare the other guesthouse for you. It's the one where David has been living in the past years, so I hope that these arrangements are suitable to you."

"They are, but I wouldn't want to take another man's house from right under them."

"David won't mind. He's a soldier, and has been one for his whole life. I'll find him temporary accommodation somewhere else," Gaspard said. "After all, you're not going to stay here for very long, are you?"

"We'll see. That depends entirely on how useful my time here will be to prepare materials for my report," Roger noted.

3. Punished

There was a painting on a wall. A rough painting filled with things to look at, small houses and trees and people and farmyard fences and the occasional animal thrown in. The perspective was off, and at parts, spots of the blank white canvas glared through the thin layers of paint. Yet the whole mess had been put in neat, ornamented frames. The eyesore dominated the hallway and was impossible to miss for anyone unlucky enough to walk under it.

"Do you like it?" A voice called out.

Roger turned around. There was a woman downstairs, one with pale skin and mild, bulging eyes. A loose skirt with ornamented hems covered her plump body.

"I heard from my husband that a charming Englishman had come to visit us," she added and climbed the stairs up, "but what exactly are you doing here?"

"That's rather odd. We talked a great deal yesterday, so I think Gaspard should know very well why I'm here," Roger said. "But what's odder is that your husband never told me that he has a wife."

"Really?" she asked before pausing to catch her breath. "I was painting when you arrived, and didn't hear you coming.

Gaspard only told me about you at dinner, and you weren't there."

"I wasn't. Your housemaid brought me dinner. I ate it alone in the guest room."

"Oh, you shouldn't have to eat alone like that. We must have a proper dinner together, as soon as possible. And a ship is coming tomorrow morning to bring in fresh food and ingredients that we could use to have a dinner like that."

"The dinner sounds lovely, but no need to do so for me."

"But you're a consul. Of course we must! Although, you should probably wear something else for that," the woman lowered her voice and looked at the same shirt that Roger had worn yesterday.

"I couldn't take many spare clothes with me. I must apologize for that. It's not any more comfortable to me than it is to you."

"I didn't mean it in a negative sense. The shirt strikes you out as a more adventurous type, someone who isn't afraid to work up a sweat."

"Right," Roger said and took a moment to think on the words. "You must excuse me another time, because I didn't catch your name."

"Oh, it's Cécile, and like my husband, I've been trapped to this lousy country for the past ten years or so," the woman presented herself. "I saw you admiring the painting. Do you like it?"

"It's...bold and imaginative. I like the strong colours. It reminds me of the work done by the School of Paris."

"I've never heard of it."

Roger clicked his tongue, "It's a small, but growing arts movement that puts more emphasis on emotion, colour and shapes than slavish obedience to realism. They only formed a couple of years ago, so you might've missed out on them, being here in Congo."

"And you think my work would fit right in there?"

"Did you paint this?"

"I did. I've been painting here to kill time. There's not much else to do."

Roger hesitated for a moment before saying, "Well, yes, I think your painting would fit just fine with the School of Paris."

"Then it's a bad painting," Cécile sighed and lowered her shoulders.

"No, not at all. It's just…different from the mainstream's ideas."

"But that's not what I went for," Cécile muttered. "It's because of my tools and paints. If I were in Brussels, I'd have all the brushes, paints and canvases a woman could want to express herself. And it's not like there are many female painters anyhow. I could be someone there, but not here."

"You don't need those things to be a great painter."

"Well, they'd certainly help."

"Do you do anything else then, besides painting?"

"Well, sometimes I read fiction, and I like to sleep in late, but not much besides that."

"Maybe you could take a walk outside. Or swim by the lake? Maybe those things could help you find new inspirations for paintings?"

She gave his words a short, gurgling laugh, "There's nothing to this place. I've even gone to see the savages a couple of times, and ended up disappointed every time."

"Why is that?"

"They're so quiet that it's practically impossible to hold a conversation with any one of them, that is, if they even are at home. I think it's because they work in the fields all day. Of course, it's for their own best, but between the mud brick houses, trees and sullen Negroes, there's just nothing outside this manor that would make it worth getting mud all over your shoes."

Roger wrung his forehead and asked, "What do you mean?"

"Oh, allow me to correct myself," she backtracked. "My husband takes good care of the savages. He's given them work, and even got his hands on one missionary – not literally, of course that would just be scandalous – to civilize them. You, of course, can go and see for yourself if you find things any different."

"That's exactly my plan."

"Oh well, at least I have my easel to content myself with," she said and shifted her legs.

"For what it's worth, Mrs Bunschoten…that's your surname, is it not?"

"It is," she said and stopped.

"I can relate to your feeling. I've spent the last three years or so in Boma, and most of it has been dreadfully boring compared to the work that I've done in the Upper Congo region in the past two months."

"Oh, you're from Boma?"

"Yes, that's where the British consulate is found."

"There's a steamer that comes here every three weeks, and goes to Leopoldville. The next ship is bound to arrive in two weeks, and I'm planning to visit."

"Do you go often?"

"Every time."

"Every time?" Roger amazed. "Even if the town is little more than a garrison with some piers and a railway station attached to it."

"I'm not staying there, of course. I take the train to coast, and then a ship to Boma. The whole trip takes just eleven days to complete."

"You go through all that trouble just to get to Boma, as often as possible?"

"I do. I have a few friends there, other unlucky wives of officials who were forced to come to Congo with their husbands. They are my only little rays of sunshine in this damp place. And Boma has all the charm of a European city. There's the two-storied hotel and restaurant, the church and the bookstore where I always get something new to read, both to myself and to Gaspard," she listed. "A month ago, there were celebrations for the Free State's anniversary."

"I know. I unfortunately happened to miss out on them because of my work."

"Oh, you absolutely should've been there. Besides the banquets, shooting contests and fireworks, there was a native orphan choir. The little dolls sang like angels."

"I'm already starting to feel regret."

"I spend a little over two weeks at a time in Boma, and come back here every time to make sure that my husband hasn't ruined things around here. This place needs a woman's touch after all," she laughed, "or at least that's what one of my friends says. I don't really know what she means by that."

"That's all very impressive, I must say."

"All of it's worth it knowing that I'll get back to civilization and for a moment can forget the misery that

Gaspard dragged me into," she said and then placed her hand gently on Roger's arm. "You know, it's actually odd that I've never seen you before in Boma. You'd think that I'd have noticed such a tall and handsome gentleman there."

"Thank you for the flattery."

"Perhaps now that you're here, there's no need for me to visit Boma the next time."

"I…appreciate the lady's words," Roger said and pulled his arm away, "but I'm here strictly for my work, and will continue on after I've gathered everything I need from here."

Before Cécile had a chance to say anything, a door was opened downstairs. Two pairs of boots stomped on creaking planks, and a voice called out for Roger. He recognized it as Henrik's from yesterday.

"Apologies, Mrs Bunschoten, but I must go now."

She fell quiet and remained behind. When Roger had almost made his way to the end of the stairs, she turned around and hollered after him, "Oh, you never told me what your work is about. You must join us for dinner and tell me all about it!"

"I will. You have my promise on that."

* * *

Sometimes it rained so much in Northern Congo during summertime that clothes and bed sheets never truly dried and retained a constant damp feel to them. The humidity could be smelt in the air, seen as drops weighing down leaves, and felt as mud under one's boots. Night rain had turned yesterday's relatively dry ground into a mire of dense mud and ponds.

"This village we're going to, what was its name again?" Roger asked.

"Bomenga," David answered.

"Is the road going to be like this the whole way?"

"Yes, all three kilometres of it. There's not much to see apart from the cultivations."

"I should've stayed at Bikoro," Henrik grumbled from behind.

"You're not afraid to dirty your boots, are you?"

"No, I'm just tired."

"If you're not feeling that well, you can stay behind and let me take Mr Casement to where he needs to be."

"No, I'm just tired, I already told you."

"There's no need to push yourself."

"I'm not pushing myself," Henrik grumbled. "Walking there in this muck will wake me up. Might as well come along to see what a consul's work is like."

Plantations flanked the road on both sides. Several dozen locals worked there. Most of them just ignored them, but occasionally a head or two popped up, and gave the two white men and their armed escort a quick glance before sinking back down into the bushes. The old, muzzle-loaded rifle thrown around David's shoulder was all the enticement they needed to not inquire into the matter further.

"Most of these men speak very little French, so you shouldn't even bother trying to talk to them," David assured to Roger. "You'd only end up wasting your time watching them scratch their heads."

"Unlike you."

"Yes, unlike me."

"Gaspard said that your command of French is excellent, and he wasn't wrong. You speak it even better than I do. Sometimes I stumble with the pronunciation, or say the English equivalent of the word I want to say, but that doesn't happen to you."

"Thank you, sir."

"It's almost extraordinary. Where did you learn to speak French so well?"

"It's a long story. Telling it would take more time than there's distance to the village," David told and pointed in the distance. "Look, you can even make out its silhouette by now."

"I'd like to hear the short version of your story."

"Well, I was an orphan that the Belgians took in. They cared for me, fed me, and trained me to become a soldier. Then they made me a corporal, and here I am now."

"You know that's a shitty story," Henrik commented.

Roger ignored the interruption and asked David, "Do you like it then? Being a soldier?"

"I do."

"Are you saying that just because you haven't known any alternative?"

"Well, there aren't many alternative types of employment in Congo for a man like me," David said and nodded towards the fields. "And at the end of the day, I'd rather be here, walking on this road, instead of working there and picking up coffee beans with my bare hands."

"In all honesty, I don't think I could do what you're doing."

"What do you mean? To be a soldier?"

"Yes."

"You wouldn't want to serve your country?"

"No, that's something that I'm already doing as a consul," Roger said. "I mean that I wouldn't want to kill for my country, for the English."

"Aren't you English?"

"No, I'm an Irishman."

"I've never heard of the Irish."

"The easiest way would be to think Ireland as what Congo is to Belgium. As such, I wouldn't want to kill for the English. But you wouldn't hesitate to do so for the Belgians?"

"Being a soldier isn't just about being willing to kill and die on a field. It's also about being willing to protect what you and others have built, and what that represents."

"So you admire the Belgians?"

"I do, yes. I'm proud of what I'm doing because the Belgians have given Congo so much. They've showed us that the world is much larger than what my ancestors would've thought it to be. And the Belgians have given us technology, education, medicine, culture, among other things," David told. "That's all worth fighting for."

"That would be an admirable reason, and I'm interested in seeing how much of it holds water."

"What about you, Mr Casement? Are you proud of the British?"

"That is a much more difficult question, and something that I don't have a clear answer to. In a certain way, yes, or otherwise I wouldn't be working for them. They gave Ireland much, but also took away much, maybe even more than what they gave."

"Like what?"

"Like culture and language. There was a time when most Irish could speak our own tongue that was distinct from both French and English, but hardly anyone speaks it nowadays."

"I don't know if that's important. French is the only language I've ever known, and I don't feel like I'm missing out on anything. It's the opposite, really, because it lets me share in with the wider world."

"Just be careful that the Belgians don't take away too much of Congo already had."

David entertained a short laugh, "No need to worry about that. Congo had nothing to it before the Belgians. They didn't take anything away."

Roger contented himself with a short hum and turned his eyes towards the approaching village. It was little more than a collection of shallow-roofed straw huts lining a mud-soaked road. There weren't many people around either. Most were away to work in the fields, but a group of men sat by one of the huts and shovelled lumps of cassava into their mouths from a shared bowl. Across the street, one man slouched on a hut's porch. He was sick, David explained, and should be avoided.

Their coming nevertheless didn't went by unnoticed. The dining men followed the newcomers with their eyes, unsure of what to make out of the unexpected guests. Heads popped out of windows and men appeared by doors, and the more they walked through the village, the more followers they gathered. Most shared two defining features: they were young, and had visible bones and joints underneath their dark skin.

One of them hollered something, words that gathered nods in the crowd. Then few of the men pointed in a certain direction, off the main village road.

"Great, as if I needed every Negro in town to see me ill," Henrik muttered.

"I think they want to show us something," Roger said. "David, do you know what they're saying?"

"I don't."

"You don't speak their language at all?"

"No. I just told you that as far as I'm concerned, French is my mother tongue."

"Well, then, do you think we should follow them?"

"If you're worried about your safety, there's no need," David smirked. "They'd never lay a hand on Henrik or me, or anyone with us."

Whatever their destination might've been, whether they wanted to go there or somewhere else, it was impossible to stop now. The crowd sucked them in and led them forward with shouts and gestures until they arrived by a hut. A hut on whose porch sat a boy. In his left hand, he held a stump of what remained of his right arm. It was here that the crowd stopped and fell quiet.

It took a moment for Roger to stutter, "What…what happened to you?" The boy looked at him with round eyes and said nothing.

Roger wrung his face and then spoke a few words in a different tongue. It was the same language he had heard the locals speak to one another, or at least the one he hoped to be the correct one based on the few words he had been able to recognize. This time the boy answered after some thought, but the words passed by Roger's ears.

Someone stepped forward from the crowd. A man who missed both hands. He presented his stumps without timidity, said something and took his place by the boy. His words had the same effect on Roger's understanding as the boy's.

"I've already told you, Mr Casement, the people here don't speak French," David almost whispered to his ear. "You shouldn't waste your time staring at them any longer."

"Waste my time? How is it a waste of time to ask someone how he ended up losing his hand?" Roger almost snapped and turned to Henrik. "Would you know anything about them?"

"All I know is that they've been here for as long as I've been here."

"And how long have you been here?"

"A year, a bit more, and to be honest, I wish I'd just stayed in Sweden," Henrik said. "Don't know anything else other than that, David is right. We should go. I don't want to waste any more time being ogled by these Negroes."

Something drew the crowd's attention. Someone else approached them, someone the locals made room for. A short, frail man dressed in a white robe and brim hat emerged from the crowd. He walked with a stoop and leaned in on a short walking cane, and behind a pair of eyeglasses his eyes looked in opposite directions, the right eye being locked towards his nose.

"You must be reason for the commotion that's going on here," the short man muttered into his long, black beard. He nodded at Henrik and David, and then turned his left eye to Roger and said, "I've never seen you before. Are you the British consul I heard about just recently?"

Roger affirmed his assumption, and asked if the man in turn was the missionary that Gaspard had mentioned to him.

"I am indeed. I'm Lucas, Lucas Peerenboom," the missionary presented himself. He reached out with his right arm and leaned in forward against his cane. Roger took hold of the hand and gave it a gentle shake.

"Do you know the reason for why I'm here?"

"I do. Gaspard already instructed me to help you with your work, however I can."

"Most missionaries know the local language of their area. Can you ask the people around why they brought us here? I know it has to do with the boy and the man missing their hands, but when I tried to ask them myself, I…"

"You don't speak Bangi, of course. Few Europeans would humiliate themselves that way."

Roger nodded. Lucas then exchanged words with the locals before saying, "They think you are like me."

"A missionary?"

"Yes, someone who might perhaps care to listen to them. They wanted to show you what happened to these two people."

"That their hands were cut off…"

"They were, during the previous government official's tenure."

"Are they the only people who went through something like that, or are they the only two left?"

"To my understanding there were never many cases to begin with, and the man and the boy are the only two left in this village from that time. Others have, since then, died."

"Then, I'd like to hear their stories," Roger said and slipped out a small notebook and a pencil. "To record their words for posterity."

"Of course."

The boy lost his hand some five years ago, Lucas told, in the last months of the rubber terror. His parents were killed, although he didn't know why, and he was wounded by a bullet. He lost his consciousness, and regained it when someone grasped him. His right hand was cut off, but the boy didn't resist, as he feared he would've been killed otherwise.

The man, in turn, had been tied to a tree and left to a torrent, after some soldiers had gone on a wanton spree of murder, and captured him without reason. His hands had swollen and the tight robes had bit all the way to the bone. Soldiers, Congolese like him, had smashed his hands off with rifle butts, while a white officer watched on and drank wine some distance away. The soldiers told him what they did was an act of mercy, but more than likely, it was instead done for the white man's amusement.

If both accounts weren't based on real events, Roger wrote, with scars of said deeds in front of him, they would've been easy to dismiss as one-dimensional stories meant only to demonize the perpetrators. With that thought, Roger put down his pencil and breathed deep.

The crowd watched in silence. Roger fiddled his fingers for a moment before mentioning, "I asked Gaspard a question that I'd also like to ask from you."

"You can ask me anything."

"In the last two years, there's been an outrage back in Europe and North America over reports of abuse like this. I've seen several pictures of handless people before, but it's never really the same as seeing something like that with your own eyes."

"It isn't, no."

"Most of the pictures have been taken by missionaries. What do you make out of them, and why do you think these reports have only now gathered attention in Europe?"

"These things happened several years ago, but with the speed that news float down from Upper Congo to Europe, I'm not surprised it has taken considerable time for these news to see daylight."

"Gaspard told me he took over five years ago, and that he ended the practice."

"He did. I was stationed here soon after he was put in charge, and thank God, I've never witnessed such brutality."

"What if he has done so, behind your back?"

Lucas dismissed the idea, "Gaspard is a businessman. He might be distant at times, but he would never abuse his workers in such a way. And a good shepherd would note if one if his lambs were sheared."

"That is a promising development, but do you know if the same holds true for the rest of the Free State?" Roger asked. "Gaspard couldn't say, but perhaps your contacts to other missionaries would."

"I rarely leave this place, given my…limitations," Lucas said and spread his arms to the sides, "and I cannot speak for the Protestants, but the few other Roman Catholics I've met have never spoken of such things."

"Well, what about the locals then? Have they ever spoken to you of these things taking place?"

"We just spoke with them. You should already know that the answer to that is also a no."

"You did, but I didn't. Gaspard mentioned that you teach the locals French," Roger recalled. "There must at least be someone in the crowd who knows enough French to hold a conversation."

"Well, there's my personal aide…"

"Which one is he? Could I speak to him?"

"I will ask his opinion on the matter first," Lucas said and turned to a man behind him. He asked him something in the local language.

The man gave a small nod before taking a careful step forward. He stood plank straight, held his arms together, and looked down, afraid that he might turn into stone if he so much as lifted his chin up by a notch. Like everyone else in the crowd, the only clothing article he had was a dirty loincloth to cover what nature had given him. He looked older than most others. Perhaps he had also been strong in his youth, but the only reminder of that now, were his broad shoulders. The visible ribcages below them told that he was just as hungry as the others.

"What's your name?" Roger asked.

"Alphonse, sir."

"No, Alphonse," Lucas interrupted. "Haven't we talked about this before? It's 'Alfons'. Your name's pronounced 'Alfons'. You need to drop the last letter 'e'. I know that proper French pronunciation takes time to learn, but you should've learned that by now."

The man just stood there and didn't say anything. Roger broke the awkward silence by asking if the man was born with that name.

"No, sir, Alphonse isn't my real name," the man said and again mispronounced his name. "Then what is your real name?"

The man glanced at Lucas. He was returned a nod.

"It's Nsala, sir," the man said. "My name's Nsala, but the father christened me Alphonse, sir."

"I see. Do you share the same mother language as the man and the boy?"

"I do, sir."

"Did Lucas leave anything out of the translation?"

"No, sir. He speaks Bangi near flawlessly."

Roger wrote down his comment, and continued, "Do you help Lucas with his work?"

"I do, sir."

"Do you like your work?"

"I do, sir. The father has always been kind to us, although..." the man said and suddenly fell silent.

"Yes, what is it?"

The man said nothing. He looked at Lucas again, who said after some hesitation, "Despite the tremendous progress that Gaspard has made in the past five years, there are still some leftovers from before."

"What do you mean?"

"It's easier to show than to explain," Lucas took over. "Come, I might as well show it to you now. It will help you see how far we've come in a short time."

* * *

A soldier, dressed like David, sat on a foldable chair with an old rifle resting over his thighs. He was there to guard a dozen wooden poles set in a row. Six of them were empty, while chains attached to an iron collar tied four men to the remaining.

Their bones shone through their dark skin, and one had broad scars marking his tights. The men hunched on the muddy ground and sewed small rugs. They seemed unaware of their surroundings, like some torpid machines repeating the same, monotonous task.

Only one of them stopped his labour and raised his head to meet the newcomers. His unmoving, petrified face was little more than protruding bone and dark crevices. His open eyes darted around, but didn't appear to register anything. He might've as well been asleep like the others, unaware of the flies buzzing around his neck. Soon his head fell back down to slumber.

"What's the meaning of this?" Roger demanded.

"They're…detained here," Lucas explained, "locals who haven't managed to fill their labour quota, working on menial labour until…"

"Is this what Gaspard meant when he told of his intentions to rebuild the broken bonds of trust between you and the locals?"

"I know it might not look pretty, but five years ago, these men would've lost their hands, like the boy and the man you just met. Instead now, they're merely being put to chains."

"Unbelievable," Roger said. "You're a man of the church. Do you really support this? How can you even stand something like this?"

"It's not really different from what you'd find in the slums and back alleys of cities back home. I know it, because I got to see the worst those places have to offer, before I found the church's light."

"That's a slim excuse."

"It's a necessary evil. A parent must be willing to use both the carrot and the stick to teach his children."

"I don't think God was the one who told you that."

"I've...I've spoken with Gaspard about this before," Lucas admitted.

"And has he taken to listen to those concerns?"

"Not really."

"Then all the grand words he spoke to me, or you for that matter, mean little when something like this goes on," Roger scoffed. His usual flat voice had taken on a tinge of anger that hadn't been there before.

He stepped out of the crowd, kneeled down in the mud by one of the chained men, and took a flask of water from his belt. The guard stood up and squeezed the rifle in his hands, while the crowd observing the scene became animated at the sight.

"You should just leave them," Henrik said.

"Why?" Roger asked and lifted the chained man's head up.

"I mean...isn't a consul's job just to be representable, look at things, and write about them?"

"You just want to leave this place a bit earlier to get some sleep, don't you?"

"What? No, it's not that."

"You could've just stayed behind and slept while ignoring these people."

"It's not that," David said. "What Henrik and Lucas said is true. This is not something that you should get bogged down in."

"Yeah, exactly that."

The prisoner appeared barely conscious, but the conversation around him brought some semblance of awareness to him. The moment his eyes passed by the flask, a sharp focus took hold of them. He rasped something.

"Water, sir," Nsala said. "He asks for the water you have."

Roger allowed the man to drink his fill. When he lifted up the flask, the prisoner clasped his hands around it, and Roger eventually had to yank it free before moving.

"Part of my job is also to help people," Roger said while fitting the flask on the next prisoner's lips. "When I'm done here, I'll go have another word with Gaspard. And if all three of you think it's inappropriate to give water to somebody who's thirsty, you should just be ashamed of yourselves."

4. Heavier Hand

Gaspard sat on a cushioned wicker chair on the mansion's porch, just outside the living room. He didn't see Roger approaching. Otherwise he would've let go of Julienne's hand before Roger called him by name, and she wouldn't have had to jerk herself free with a gasp.

"Mr Casement, you surprised me," Gaspard said aloud before turning to Julienne and shooing her away. "Why don't you go back to the garden and tend to the weeds."

"I'm sorry, sir, what did you want me to do?" Roger heard her mutter. "Just go."

Julienne nodded, turned away and left.

"So, Mr Casement," Gaspard said, stood up and stroked his jacket as if to brush off all the unpleasant business Roger had just seen. "Have you toured the plantation's surroundings today?"

"I have, indeed."

"And? How have you found our little slice of civilization?"

"My first impressions have been less than desirable."

Gaspard's mouth opened from surprise. It took him a moment to ask what Roger meant.

"I visited Bomenga like you suggested. Most of the locals however, seemed hungry and sick, and four men had been tied to wooden poles by chains."

"I don't really see how these things are of concern."

"I see them as a concern, and I'm sure the British parliament will view them the same."

"Perhaps spending the last three years in Boma has made you blind to see just how challenging the Upper Congo region is to develop. The rainy season makes agriculture difficult, and diseases wreak death on both sides. There are barely some eighty steamers operating in the Congo river, both by the state and private companies, and they need to cross distances measured in thousands of kilometres," Gaspard defended. "With all this considered, I'm doing the best I can with what little I have."

"How do the chains factor into it all?"

"Tell me, Mr Casement, have you ever spent much time with children?"

"I haven't had the privilege."

"If you had, then you'd know that there are two ways to guide a child: by showing example, and if that doesn't work, by chastising them. The natives here are no different from children in that regard. The chains are simply a necessary evil for the stubborn few that need a stick instead of a carrot to learn."

"Lucas said almost the exact same thing."

"Then he understands the importance of that lesson."

"Then can you tell me who these stubborn few who refuse to learn are?"

"Natives, who failed to collect their quotas of products, owned by the Free State around Lake Mantumba," Gaspard explained and motioned his arm in a wide arc. "I have a rule that one man from an offending village is detained for every ten missing rations from each bi-weekly quota. It's up to the natives themselves to decide who takes the blame."

"Is that also your idea of teaching them democracy?"

"You could see it that way. It's not harsh by any means,"

"That depends on your understanding of harsh, and on how the prisoners are punished for their 'crimes'."

"The men are not prisoners," Gaspard emphasized. "They're merely detained until some sort of satisfaction can be obtained from them. They work as carpet weavers until their villages can provide the missing labour or produce. Failing that, the men are conscripted into the army, as no able-bodied man should go to waste if they can provide something of value instead."

"All this sounds scantly legal to me. On what grounds, do you base these rules?"

"I'm only following the Free State's constitution to the best of my abilities. It's impossible to get lawyers all the way here, never mind a court of justice. And detainment is the most humane form of punishment anyway. It doesn't hurt the person, only makes them uncomfortable and to feel shame."

"Have you seen those prisoners in Bomenga? They were outright suffering."

"Without our efforts, Mr Casement, the Africans would forever remain as ignorant primitives. They cannot help themselves, and therefore need to be guided, sometimes with a heavier hand."

"Need?"

"If necessary. Africans know no other law but that of the strongest and no other form of coercion than intimidation. What I'm doing here is only to improve their condition, so that instead of clapping their hands and stomping their feet all day, they're hard at work, just like proper Europeans back home. And work is, after all, the building block of civilization."

"Your chains are nothing more than the cold, grasping hand of Leopold," Roger objected. "All of it just sounds like a thinly veiled excuse to justify one man's vision of frontier justice."

"Mr Casement, I wouldn't expect such theatrics from a consul, if you even are one with the lacklustre documents you have to show for it," Gaspard said. "Therefore, I ask you to retain your tongue, or I'll make a formal complaint of your behaviour to the governor-general."

Roger backed down. He let down his shoulders and breathed out, "Apologies."

"Apology accepted. I can understand how visiting Upper Congo is not the same as living here for years and getting used to the realities of life so far away from civilization. My wife's initial reaction was the same in the months after we arrived. Nowadays she's just indifferent."

Roger fell quiet for a moment, not really sure how to take the words. If they were meant as an insult to coax him further, or simply as a smug observation. He decided not to dwell on the words and moved on, "What of the others then, the locals who aren't detained: what compels them to work?"

"Public duty, believe it or not. It's perfectly fair that the natives should contribute towards the country's administration cost. Otherwise they're free men and sovereign citizens of his majesty's realm, and we pay them compensation for the produce they bring in."

"You said that the produce doesn't belong to the locals, but to the Free State who owns the soil itself. How then do you buy from them what's already yours?"

"We don't buy the produce. We pay the natives compensation for collecting and bringing in the Free State's property that grows on its land."

"Based on the ledgers that I went through yesterday, you pay the locals in the usual brass rods."

"I do."

"But the compensation doesn't appear to be very much."

"Regrettably. To make up for it, the natives are also paid in everyday European items, such as cloth, strings and buttons."

"Isn't the latter odd considering that the locals don't wear anything more than loincloths?"

"They've yet to grasp the concept of sewing proper clothes," Gaspard said. "Fair labour must be compensated by something, anything that happens to be at hand. I think you agree with that. Again, I'm only doing the best I can in light of the situation."

"Well, at least what I saw today didn't match the worst reports of abuse I've heard, although I also happened to meet a boy and a man who ended up losing their hands during the closing months of the rubber terror."

"Did you also meet Father Lucas?"

"I did, and he was generous enough to translate the victims' stories to me."

"Very good. I outlawed that barbarous practice the moment Bikoro was entrusted to me, as I explained earlier. And having met them, I think you might see how my methods are preferable over wanton slaughter that the previous official was so fond of."

"They're barely an improvement."

"We have to respectfully disagree on that," Gaspard said.

David appeared out of the other guest room, the one Roger wasn't using, at the other end of the courtyard. He had helped Henrik to rest there after their visit to Bomenga.

Gaspard looked at him with pride, much like a father would look at his child for excelling at school. He told how David was a prime example of grasping what he had just explained.

David made his way across the courtyard to see Julienne who went through the small garden's vegetables absent-mindedly. He greeted her and leaned in on the picket fence. She took her mind off of the plants, stood up and returned him the courtesy. They chatted in simple French, and it was then that the smile on Gaspard's lips faded.

"There's also one final thing," Roger's words snapped him out of it. "I met a local who went by the name Alphonse. Or at least, that's what Lucas had named him. He told me his original name was Nsala."

"I don't think I've met him, or if I have, I don't remember anyone by those names. Who is he?"

"The father's assistant."

"I see. No wonder why he gave him a French name, because I've no idea how to write or pronounce that other name," Gaspard commented. "What makes him so special then? Lucas has never mentioned him to me before."

"I can't comment on the latter, but he speaks French fairly well, not on the same level as David, but much better than

Julienne. Having him here by my side could prove useful for my work."

"Why not just talk with David instead?"

"He's not much of a conversationalist. An army career man, through and through."

"Can't blame him for that," Gaspard said. "But if this native of yours speaks French fairly well, then I could actually use him here instead of letting him hide away in Bomenga. My wife, Cécile…have you met her, by the way?"

"I did in the morning, but only passingly."

"I see. You must nevertheless already be familiar with how much she adores her brushes and books, not to mention the river steamers, instead of taking care of the house like any good wife should," Gaspard muttered as something slowly dawned on him. "Yes, that could work. This native could help both you and me."

"I, however, wouldn't want to do so without Lucas' approval." "Of course not. I'll just borrow him for a spell so that he can help you with your work. And when he's not doing that, he can help Julienne with the chores,"

Gaspard said and then hollered in the distance, "Fidèle, come here for a moment."

David stood up and made his way towards the porch. Mud splashed around his bare feet. "Yes, sir, what is it?"

"There's someone named 'Alphonse' at Bomenga," Gaspard said and glanced at Roger, who nodded. "I'd like you to go with Henrik and bring him here. The man works with Father Lucas."

"Understood, sir," David said, "although Henrik isn't doing that well."

"What do you mean?"

"I don't know, sir. I helped him to his room to get some rest, and then he told me to leave him alone. I think he's sick."

"It could be," Roger added. "He said he was just tired on the way to and back from Bomenga, but it seemed worse than that."

"I see. Let's hope whatever he's got will pass with sleep," Gaspard said and then turned back to Roger. "It wouldn't sit right with me for you to sleep in a room next to a sick man, and having to listen to his moaning all night. I can have a mattress prepared for you somewhere in the mansion instead."

"I appreciate the offer, but this shouldn't present a problem."

"As you wish," Gaspard noted and sent David on his way alone. "I think it's, however clear that we'd need much more time, with comfortable seating and refreshments, to go over your previous points and concerns in more detail."

"Cécile already invited me to share dinner with you."

"Surprisingly proactive of her. But yes, a dinner like that would be an excellent opportunity to get to know one another better. Because if we're going to be partners, then we should know one another as best as we can."

"I agree, and think that tomorrow would suit the best for that," Roger said. "We both have a shared interest for my report to look as spotless as possible, for the sake of the Free State's reputation."

"Indeed. For the sake of the Free State's reputation," Gaspard repeated with a nod. "I also hope this Alphonse of yours can cook. Julienne does, thank God, because my wife sure can't! Have you heard of such? A woman who can't tell a ladle apart from a knife?"

Roger passed a slight smile over his lips, the kind that could either be interpreted as amusement, or simply a polite gesture with no more meaning to it.

5. Father

A groping hand placed a moist towel on a man's forehead. He shivered and then coughed before a spoon hovered under his nose. The plain cassava on it didn't smell like much, not enough to wake up an appetite, but not enough to take it away either. Fingers forced his dry lips apart, planted in the spoon, and then let the mouth close in around the spoon before it slipped out. Then the same hand took hold of the jaw and moved it up and down. The slow, tedious process was all that Lucas could do for the dying man, to at least alleviate some of his pain.

He heard someone else enter the building. It was a large, spacious house, built from wood and straw to emulate something that would've been found overseas. Most of it was reserved for communal gatherings to hear the word of God, but towards the back was a smaller space reserved for the missionary's personal use. Some gaps in the walls let in late afternoon sun's rays, and were the room's only source of illumination. A large carpet took up the floor, a handful of ceramic pots could be found here and there, and a woven tower shield adorned one of the walls: they were all gifts from grateful locals to the God's anointed.

"Father, there was something I wished to discuss with you," Nsala said.

"Can you wait for a moment first, please?" Lucas asked.

"Of course."

Lucas lowered his head, placed his hands together and muttered something. A prayer for the sick. When the act was done, he removed the towel and dropped it into a bowl of brown water. Then he picked up his cane, stood up and turned around, slowly and carefully.

"The sleeping sickness is a needlessly cruel disease," he told in the local language. "First it makes one's thoughts wander astray, then turns the muscles sore, and finally sleepiness takes hold of the afflicted, until they fall into a dream from which they never wake up from. There's no cure, so all one can do is to make the passing as comfortable as possible."

Nsala gave a small nod to acknowledge his words. "Alright, Alphonse. What did you wish to talk about?"

"I wanted to talk about today's events."

"What of them?"

"What did you make out of the foreign dignitary that visited us?"

"You mean Mr Casement?" Lucas asked, and Nsala nodded. "He seemed like a reasonable man. Perhaps a little bit too driven by his emotions, but a good man nonetheless."

"I had the same impression. The way he expressed his concerns over the mutilated boy and man, and how he treated the four prisoners, were admirable. His actions also made me think."

"Think of what?"

Nsala cleared his throat before asking, "If you had never told me and the others about Christ, would we have gone to Hell?"

The question's nature caught Lucas off-guard at first, but he was quick to answer, "No, you wouldn't have gone to Hell, but neither to Heaven."

"Then why did you come here and tell us about Christ in the first place?"

"If I hadn't, then your souls would've been lost to God for all eternity. There can be no salvation for someone who doesn't accept His teachings into their heart."

"But there would neither have been damnation for us?"

"No, only emptiness and nothingness. Knowledge of Christ's word should be shared to all who have yet to hear of it. That's why I came here, to help you and the others avoid this fate, but the final decision on whether to accept God into your hearts is only up to you."

Nsala nodded and then recalled, "In one of your classes, you told how Christ suffered many injustices in life, and was eventually crucified for His beliefs."

"He died for our sins. It was His gift to us, as without His death, the gates of Heaven would've forever remained closed to us."

"But do you think what Christ went through was justified?"

"He suffered so that we shouldn't have to. Most of His contemporaries treated Him harshly, and saw Him as little more than a troublemaker."

"Then, in the same vein, do you think what's happening here is justified?"

"What are you getting at, Alphonse? You already know much of what we have gone through just now." Lucas asked and wrung his forehead. "Please, speak freely. You know I won't judge anyone."

"You said you think what happened to Christ was wrong."

"I did."

"But do you also think what happened to the maimed boy and man was wrong? Do you think that the prisoners who are tied to those posts deserve their punishment?"

Lucas pulled back his head a notch and muttered into his beard, "This is about your daughter again, isn't it?"

"It is. Do you think what your countrymen did to my daughter was…justified? Do you think that Christ would approve of such an act? Was it necessary to do that to a child? It has been months now since I even saw her the last time."

"What was done to your daughter was not justified at all, but she is still alive, isn't she? I don't approve of violence, but killing her would've been a far graver offense."

"It's still an offense."

"Sometimes the best way to do good is to choose the lesser of two evils."

"There was nothing good in any of that. It was just senseless violence," Nsala said back. "I know you're a good man at heart, sir. But you've been here with us for years now. Why have you never decided to do something about them, like the newcomer did?"

"You know I have said it to Gaspard many times that I don't approve of these things, but he has the last say on the matter."

"This Casement was brave enough to stand up to him, and he's a Christian missionary like you. Why aren't you like him?"

"He is a fellow Christian, but not a missionary. He's also from a different country, and has a different king to mine."

"Is that the reason you're not brave? Leopold isn't here in Congo to see and hear you, but Christ is. If he'd see the suffering outside, he'd never approve of it."

"No, you're wrong about that, Alphonse," Lucas said slowly. "Leopold is here in Congo with us, and one should always be wary of the snake in the garden."

"I don't understand. How is your king here with us? My tribe's chieftain is close-by, a week's distance by walking, you know this because you've met him."

"I have, yes."

"…but your king is so far away that you'd have to travel by steamboat for months to meet him."

"Alphonse, you shouldn't blame me for who God made me to be. He has His reason for every hardship and misery. You're free however, to talk to Mr Casement about your concerns, because I'm afraid I can't do much to ease them. I've already tried, and that has led me nowhere."

Nsala opened his mouth to say something, but Lucas glanced at him above his eyeglasses' left lens. The distant look troubled Nsala and made him fall quiet. There was a hint of sorrow in his wet eyes, but also a wish that he wouldn't press the matter and instead just leave him alone.

The sick man coughed. Lucas turned his attention back at him, and after stumbling over the empty air a few times, managed to place a wet towel on the man's forehead.

* * *

Nsala walked out through the back door. A small graveyard full of simple wooden crosses greeted him silently. Each cross marked one death, but not every death. The sleeping sickness was only one thing that had filled the bleak field. Exhaustion from work and hunger had also partaken in the toll, among other things.

He breathed in deep, and looked past the graveyard, at the jungle's edge. His eyes stayed there for a moment before he turned them away and left.

The wooden poles weren't far from here. The crowd around them had dispersed following the British consul's departure with the two soldiers. The small, unexpected act of kindness would've been enough for the four prisoners to lose all interest in their chores, if the lone guard and his old rifle hadn't reminded them otherwise.

Most of the mud had dried enough to become a sticky paste underneath his feet. Few pools of water remained here and there. They glimmered faintly in the setting sun's golden rays. There was more life to the village by evening, and a smell of warm cassava in the wind. People who had wasted away their day working in the fields had made it back home and gathered together to share a meal of nothing more than boiled cassava and water. Then they would head to sleep, too tired to do anything else, in the hopes that they'd get enough sleep to give their ached muscles some rest, and to make it through the next day. And the next day after that, and the next, far into the foreseeable future. None possessed enough strength to spare a shred of pity to the unfortunate few in chains, other than perhaps passingly thinking of them as a warning of what would happen to them as well if they missed their work quotas.

Nsala pitied the others, both the ones who had to break their backs in the fields and the ones in chains, but he also couldn't help but feel a forlorn sense of happiness that he didn't have to worry about that anymore. Not after that particular night when he begged for his daughter's to be spared. He had continued to beg long after the deed had been done and his daughter's silent body had been dragged away, until he had almost choked on his tears.

He hadn't slept that night at all. Instead, he had rested his head on planks, watched the pale moon from behind reed curtains and silvery clouds, and listened to the others' snoring. By morning, fuelled by nothing more than the comfort of routine, he had prepared to go back to the fields. But then the brute had come to him, his shape melting against the rising sun behind him.

The brute had told in the foreigner's tongue that he was too weak to work in the fields anymore, too frail to even protect his daughter. The brute asked if he understood. Nsala nodded. The brute then informed him that he had been given a new duty, to help the half-blind father in gaining the locals' trust, in learning the foreigner's tongue and their ways. He was to either help the merciful God's chosen, or lose his hand as well.

He chose the former. But how could he do any of that after everything he had been through?

Nsala sat on his shared house's small porch, and thought of it all. People passed by him, going on with their own lives and worries. Someone asked for him to come and share a meal with them, but he shrugged them off.

He only wanted to think. To dwell on the day's events. But he wasn't afforded the opportunity. The same brute came to him again. This time his face was lit by golden light.

"Alphonse, right?" David asked but didn't wait for an answer, "Gaspard wants you to work in his mansion from now on. Pack your things, if you have any. He wanted to see you before nightfall."

6. Thousand Sheets

A large, two-decked steamer crawled over Lake Mantumba's quiet surface in the morning. In its wake came waves that kept rolling over the surface long after the steamer had been tied to the flimsy pier that creaked under the weight of all the cargo that was brought ashore on the backs of local carriers.

Most of it were little more than everyday necessities and food, but among them came a delivery of something special, baking ingredients that Cécile had ordered from Boma some three months ago via express shipping. In return for these European delicacies, the steamer was loaded with bags of coffee and cacao beans, as well as the odd dried lumps of rubber that resembled grey, uneven glass panels.

At evening, a lone light shone from a window overlooking the dark lake. It came from the mansion's small kitchen, one that even included a small refrigerator kept operational by a constant sputtering of a small steam turbine in a closet. Julienne had spent most of the day in the kitchen preparing a dinner for Gaspard, his wife, and their new guest.

She had Nsala to help her. After being transferred to the mansion just this morning, he had received a pair of old pants and a shirt with a few holes in it, as well as a pair of sandals. The clothes were meant to make him more representable and decent, but they only felt odd to him, unnatural. Their coarse texture irritated his skin. He couldn't understand how the foreigners could stand wearing them in the day's heat, and the sensation didn't really ease with sunset. He wanted nothing more than to just rip the shirt off.

He jerked his arm to the side in an attempt to adjust the sleeve. His arm came close to hitting Julienne in the head.

"Be careful," she snapped.

"I'm sorry. It's just this shirt. How can you wear your clothes like that?"

"You get used to them in time," she said indifferently and turned her attention back to whipping cream in a bowl. "You should just keep kneading that dough, or otherwise we'll never get the pastries done in time."

"I know, I know," he said, picked up some more butter and sunk his arms back into the mix.

"You know, you're obviously new here," she said after a moment and leaned in against the kitchen table with her back. "Did you come here recently?"

"No, I've already been living in Bomenga for years."

"Oh, I see. So you're just new to the mansion then," she said and turned her attention back to whipping cream.

"Why did you ask?" he continued.

"New people arrived here yesterday, near midnight. They're from south," she explained. "I just thought you'd be one of them."

"Well, I'm from north-east," he said and was again faced with an awkward silence before he continued, "are they people you know?"

"Yes. They're from my home village."

"Did they come here looking for work?"

"No. They came here in chains."

"What? Why?" he asked and stopped working as well. "Did they fail to fill their quotas?"

"I talked to a few of them. They refused to give any food in the first place."

"That's suicide. Everyone knows what happens to those who refuse."

"It wasn't the first time," she told and kept muttering to the cream while whisking it. "The last time some soldiers burned down a few houses and pointed their guns at the chieftain who gave a few of us to them. A young white man leading the soldiers said that I was worth two, so the chieftain tossed me at them without hesitation. He was given a medal for that."

"So what happened this time, for more to end up like that?"

"It wasn't just more, it was the entire village. They didn't have any food left to give. The same chieftain told the soldiers that he needed every remaining person to work in the fields, just to keep themselves fed. It wasn't good enough for the soldiers however, so they forced him on his knees and beheaded him. Then they opened fire and killed at random."

"That's horrible. Did your family or friends make it out alive?"

"There was a childhood friend among the men I met yesterday. He told all my relatives were killed," she said without a chance in her tone and without stopping her work, like it didn't matter to her at all. "All the surviving men were put in chains, and all others were taken as prisoners to ensure that the men would work here. And then they took most of the remaining crops and livestock as a reward for all their hard work."

She held up the beater. Few beads of cream dropped from it back into the bowl while she pointed at a chunk of meat roasting over an open fire. She said, "That lamb is from my village. It was the only one the soldiers didn't eat on their way back."

"And now we're serving it to Gaspard and the foreign dignitary?" he hesitated at the thought of it. "Does he know of it?"

"The newcomer with the funny beard? Maybe, maybe not. It doesn't matter. All the foreigners are devils. Gaspard is just as much of an oppressor as the people who came before him, and the people who will come after him," she said and turned her attention back to beating the cream. "My grandmother used to tell me how the white people are dead spirits sent to torment us, and they're not leaving anytime soon."

"Your mother was a witch."

"You can call her that if you want, but she was right. The foreigners are pale, like death, they came from the sea, and they take us. She also told how they eat us. They eat the brains, drink the blood, and cure the meat for later."

"Now that's just ridiculous. They might be cruel, you're right, but they're not cannibals."

"Well, isn't their religion all about it? About eating the body of their god, and drinking his blood again and again in some perverted ritual?"

"I don't believe any of that," he dismissed. "I know the missionary here. He's a man of their god, this Christ."

"I know what a missionary is."

"Then you should also know that during those rituals they only serve bland bread and thin wine that tastes bad."

"How do you know you haven't drunk blood all that time?"

"It's symbolic, nothing more than that."

"But how do you know that?" she insisted. "Have you ever drunk blood before that?"

"It...it hasn't looked like blood."

"So you don't know what exactly they serve you in those ceremonies," she scoffed. "It could be blood of people you've known, of all the things."

"It's not blood, I'm sure of it."

She shook her head, pointed her beater towards a row of metal cans lining a shelf and said, "The few devils came here from somewhere. And if there's a whole country of them out there, then imagine how much of us they need for all of their rituals. Those cans in there are used to store all of the parts, so that they don't get spoiled on the way back."

"That's just stupid, you know that, right?"

"No. It's the truth. And they prefer our hands over everything else."

"I've never seen anyone end up in a pot, or their hands on a white person's plate."

"Of course not, they wouldn't show that to us."

"Instead," he ignored her, "what happens is that a soldier brings the hands to a white man for a reward, and then the hand is tossed to rot on the ground."

"Why would they need so many hands if they're just going to let them rot?"

Nsala placed down the dough ball and went over to the shelf. He picked up one of the cans that had a drawn picture of carrots on it and asked, "Do you really think there's hands inside of this?"

"Can you just finish making the dough and give it to me, please?" she said in an annoyed tone.

He shook his head and an uneasy silence fell in the kitchen. Julienne left the beaten cream to cool, and was handed the ready dough. She rolled it into a thin sleet, placed it between two baking sheets and then placed it inside a simple oven to bake.

Nsala couldn't shake off the conversation they had just had, and continued, "You obviously don't like the Belgians. If all of your relatives are now dead, what makes you stay here? You could escape without any consequences to people close to you."

"Because outside of this place there's nothing more than jungle and villages that have either been burned down or cannot take in another mouth to feed. At least here, I have food and water, and a place to sleep in."

Nsala hesitated for a moment before saying, "I don't like the Belgians much either, but they have my only daughter as hostage. They cut off her hand, and I saw it being dumped to a mound of dirt. That's…that's how I know what happens to the hands."

"I had no idea," she said slowly, and her tone changed. "I'm sorry."

"Thank you. I think that this new foreigner, however, this Casement, is different. It's almost like he wants to help us."

"He might appear nicer than Gaspard, but he's the same as the others."

"Have you met him?"

"Passingly. He asked me some questions in their tongue, like who I was and what I do. I couldn't understand all of it, but I know that he spends a lot of time with Gaspard. No good can come out of it."

"He asked me the same questions in Bomenga. He came there to see the crippled and the prisoners. He went so far as to give them water against the others' wishes."

"Well, that's nice of him," she said indifferently.

"I worked under the missionary I mentioned, a man named Lucas. I know he feels the same as Casement, but is too afraid of their king to act. I don't know why Casement isn't afraid of their king, but that sets him apart."

"He's just one man. Why do you think he can do anything at all for this place?"

"I don't know, to be honest, but I must at least try to speak with him and tell him about my daughter. He already asked that I'd be moved here to help him with his work. It can't be meaningless. I think he can help me see my daughter again after so much time, and to finally make sure she's safe."

"You don't know if she's safe?"

"No. But I know that she's alive. And if she weren't, I would've escaped a long time ago and taken my chances in the jungle."

"Well, I can admire that you're doing all this for someone else."

* * *

A heavy silver plate was placed in the middle of a dining table, and a dome covering it was removed. A sliced cutlet of mutton sat in the middle of a pool of its own red juice and assorted vegetables. A beautiful bowl was placed next to it, filled to the brim with a deep brown sauce.

"It looks splendid," Roger commented the sight. "Doesn't it?" Cécile asked.

"I had the servants slaughter one of our lambs for this dinner," Gaspard added.

"You shouldn't have had to do that just for me. I'm starting to wonder if all this is even a bit too much on your behalf."

"Oh, there's never anything exciting going on in Congo, so your charming presence gives all the reason for a celebration," Cécile said, and then turned to Henrik. "As well as yours, good Henrik. I hope you get better soon."

Henrik sat at the other end of the table, slouched deep into his chair. His short, blonde hair had somehow managed to get into a tousle. The two uppermost buttons on his plain white shirt were open, and revealed reddish skin under the faint gleam of sweat. He looked away, coughed and then muttered his thanks to the cutlet under a laboured breath.

"I hope the food will make you feel better, young man," Gaspard said with a shy smile. "Do you still know what has gotten into you?"

Henrik shook his head.

"It could be anything, really," Roger mentioned. "Most likely it's malaria."

"How would you know?" Henrik rasped.

"I've had it three times myself."

Henrik tried to give his words a laugh, but only ended up coughing over his plate. "Does it get easier the more you get it?"

"Not really. I had my third case little over a year ago, and I had to postpone my work here because of it. One shouldn't take malaria lightly," Roger told. "On the other hand, dysentery or typhoid fever could also be what's ailing you."

"I hope it's not dysentery," Henrik muttered. "I wouldn't want to shit blood-soaked diarrhoea all over the place."

"Now, I, for my part, wouldn't want to discuss these matters at a table," Cécile said.

"I agree," Gaspard said. "I only hope that you'll enjoy the meal, both of you."

Henrik stayed quiet, and so Roger thanked in his stead, "I'm sure of it. I'm not much of a cook myself, to be honest. The boy piloting the steamer, I arrived here in, said to me that he's also a cook, but he can't prepare anything other than chicken and custard with too much sugar to it for the life of his."

"That sounds even more horrible than the usual all too one-sided food we eat here," Cécile entertained a laugh.

"Well, you have to make do with what you have on the road. I haven't had proper vegetables in a long time. Are the ones on offer from your garden as well?"

"They are."

"They look delicious. You are lucky to have your own garden out here."

"We are, although it's nowhere near as large as I'd want it to be. More variety is what it needs. The surrounding villages pitch in and bring in some fresh food and meat and fish, but most days there's little more on offer than that awful tasteless mass that the natives call food. I tell you, the food here gets dreadfully boring and fast."

"You get used to cassava over time," Gaspard noted. "At least, it keeps the hunger away."

"At least it keeps the hunger away," Cécile repeated with a scoff. "Did you hear that, dear Casement? And that's what I'm supposed to eat daily."

"All the more reason to celebrate tonight, then."

"You're right," she said and passed her finger across the rim of her wine glass. "Did you know that this wine is also from Europe? They told me it's the same one that everyone drinks in Paris these days."

"Also? Is there something else on tonight's menu that's imported besides the wine?"

"Hmm, you'll just have to wait and see. Suffice to say, it's my favourite food," she said in a playful tone, leaned in and rested her chin on both of her hands. Her stomach bulged against the table. Then she turned her attention to Julienne standing by the wall and said to her in a cold tone, "That reminds me that you should return to the kitchen and make sure the food's prepared to perfection."

Julienne didn't lift her head up, but it was clear that she hadn't fully understood what had been said. Nsala whispered to her the translation without lifting his eyes from the floor either, after which she bowed hastily, apologized, and left the room.

"Well, should we begin the meal before it gets cold?" Gaspard asked.

"Of course," Roger said and gestured towards the mutton. "I think Henrik should go first."

"Good idea."

Gaspard had to call Henrik by name twice and snap his fingers over the meal before he stirred from his half-slumber. He groaned and looked at the cutlet with empty eyes.

"Let me help you with that, sir," Nsala said, bowed and stepped forward.

Henrik didn't object to the offer, and allowed him to cut a slice of the cutlet for him. Nsala also made sure to place some vegetables on his plate, and asked how much Henrik wanted the sauce. He only asked for a bit.

"How is Nsala settling in?" Roger asked.

"Alphonse, you mean? Good, I think," Gaspard answered. "Father Lucas didn't have anything to say against the matter."

"I didn't get a say in this either," Cécile protested. "In the end, I'm the one in charge of this household, and I say we don't need another servant. Julienne is already bad enough at her job. How would this new one be any different?"

"I only need him here for a week. Two at most," Roger said. "I think his fluency in both French and the local language makes him invaluable for my work."

Nsala put the sauce bowl back in place and made his way to Gaspard. He gestured towards the mutton.

"Oh, no. You should serve my dear wife before me." Nsala bowed to apologize his breach of protocol.

"Well, he lacks knowledge of the proper etiquette," Cécile muttered. "Just like Julienne."

"You must forgive him the small mistakes. Otherwise he appears natural in this role, and a quick learner with initiative," Gaspard said with a content nod. "It's good that he knows his place. And if he keeps up the good work, I think I might just keep him around."

"You don't think Lucas would mind?" Roger asked.

"Not at all. Julienne has her uses, but her timidness and lack of acumen for French holds her back. Besides, a small mansion like this suits a man of Alphonse's talents much better than some makeshift church."

Cécile remained silent while Nsala slowly but surely prepared her meal on her plate. After her, Roger was the next to be served. The host of the evening left himself as last. The smell of the freshly cut mutton had stirred the bulldog John's attention. He poked at his master's feet and attempted to climb into his lap. Roger chucked him a piece of meat absent-mindedly.

The dining room wasn't very large, just large enough to accommodate the oval-shaped wooden table that had enough space around it for six chairs. Four were in use now, but it looked like only three had ever been used. Wall-mounted candles illuminated the room on all sides. A large painting of what looked like a wild leopard or some other big cat hiding in a dense forest dominated the wall behind Cécile and Gaspard. It was difficult to say for certain what animal hid in the work, as only its comically over-sized red eyes and tail were visible, but it was clear that its creator sat below it.

Cécile brought up some small-talk while they dined. Sometimes she spoke with her mouth full, and Roger and Gaspard both contented themselves with simple replies and nodding. Henrik abstained from joining in the conversation and focused entirely on nibbling tiny bits from his food.

Roger glanced at Nsala a few times. He had assumed his original position near the kitchen door. He stood there with his head held down, but it was obvious that he felt uncomfortable. He constantly shifted in place and moved his shoulders around carefully, but otherwise only stirred when Gaspard asked for more wine, or Cécile for more meat.

When the others had mostly finished their meals, Henrik placed his serviette onto the table with a sigh and pushed the plate away. He apologized, "You'll have to excuse me, Mr and Mrs Bunschoten, but I'm still not feeling well."

"Oh, you poor thing, there's nothing to apologize for in your state," Cécile said. "Do you feel like you should go lie down?"

"Yes, yes, I think that would be good," Henrik managed to say behind his laboured breath.

"My dear wife is right. If you feel like you should leave us and go rest, you should do so. Good food alone can't cure you."

"I...yes, apologies," Henrik said and tried to push his chair away from the table. "Thank you for the invitation, in any case."

Roger was about to help him stand up, but Nsala was faster.

"Let me help you, sir."

Henrik looked up with watered eyes. They stopped at his face and lingered there, as if Henrik wasn't quite sure who the man was anymore. Then he nodded and stood up with a grunt. Nsala offered to escort him to his guest house, but Henrik shook him off indifferently: he was weak, but still stubborn enough to refuse further help.

As he left, Nsala pushed the chair back into its place, folded the serviette and picked up the plate that still had some food on it. Gaspard watched him with a glint in his eyes. He commented, "My instinct was right about you, young man: you will make for an excellent servant."

Nsala thanked him passingly before passing the plate to the kitchen. Roger waited for him to come back and assume the same position he had held for most of the evening before he wiped the corners of his mouth with a serviette. Then he brought up, "I've been thinking lately, Mr Bunschoten."

"You think a lot," Gaspard noted and took a gulp from his wine glass.

"It's my job."

"Well, what have you thought of now?"

"Like Cécile said, isn't one servant already enough for you? Why keep another one around?"

Gaspard gave his words a dry laugh, "With how much time my dear wife spends away from here, I'm afraid not, despite what she says about this place needing a woman's touch."

"Gaspard," she flinched, "that was rude."

"It's the truth, dear. Julienne has had a hard time keeping up with all the household work because you don't partake in it. Another servant would make things run smoother around here."

"What of my paintings then? Don't they liven up the place?"

He glanced over his shoulder and said, "Your paintings cannot keep the dust or the hunger away. And I think the only place where you'd find appreciation for them is in the underbelly of Paris."

Cécile huffed, and Roger backtracked, "So far you've struck me as someone who prefers to do things by yourself, and by his own rules. A case of point being your ledgers. So why not take care of the house yourself?"

"Because I already have a lot of work to do, such as the aforementioned ledgers. There are also better suited hands available to do the more menial tasks."

"Do you mean Cécile, or the locals by that?"

"Both. And besides, the work that Alphonse would do here offers him an unparalleled front-row seat to see the benefits that the Free State can give to its citizens. Work is also an important part in bringing the natives to Christ's flock, and I'm sure Lucas can appreciate that."

"You seem so certain of these benefits."

"That's because our work can only benefit the natives."

"The white man's burden," Roger spelled out.

"Yes. We Europeans have an outright duty to seize Africa for ourselves. If the natives had achieved on their own what we did back in Europe, then there wouldn't be a need for either of us – for any of us three – to be here in the middle of nowhere for them," Gaspard said and corrected himself with a cough.

"If I remember correctly, it were the Portuguese who 'discovered' Congo some four hundred years ago. Back then there was a kingdom here, one of the largest in Africa."

"I've heard of it, M'banza Kongo or some such ineligible mumble. However it might be, the kingdom was weak and fell to the Portuguese in short time. Nowadays it's nothing but a sad memory of its past, hunched somewhere near the border with Angola," Gaspard told. "In its place, we now have a strong centralized state that can only benefit the inhabitants of this land."

"From everything that I've seen so far in Upper Congo paints a different picture."

"Is it? We've improved the infrastructure, built schools, hospitals and churches, taught the natives one shared language, and told them of God's kingdom. And we've freed the locals from slavery," Gaspard said. It sounded to Roger like he was included in all of that development.

"Well, if there's one thing that Leopold should be commended for, it's that the slave trade in Upper Congo is nowadays extinct," Roger said and looked elsewhere, reluctant to admit anything else on the matter.

"Right. You said you were here sixteen years ago. You must've seen it with your own eyes."

"I did, yes."

"Oh, you never told me about that," Cécile said. "What were your impressions on it?"

"What? On slavery? It's horrible of course."

"It is," Gaspard took over as Cécile's face turned pale at the realization of what exactly she had blurted out. "Some Arab slavers still lurk in the country's easternmost parts, but they'll soon be eradicated once and for all."

"I remember how the inhabitants of Upper Congo paddled their way downstream, all the way to the Livingstone Falls near today's Leopoldville, where they sold their countrymen to other locals and foreigners in exchange for trinkets and booze."

Gaspard nodded with content, leaned forward and smacked his lips. He continued in a lower voice, "Even worse still was the sale of humans as meat. I've heard of cannibalism among primitive peoples before, but never of something like that anywhere else in the world. Did you see something like that as well? Marketplaces where tied up humans were sold like cattle."

"Dear," Cécile interrupted, "on second thought, I…I wouldn't want to talk about this on the table."

"Apologies. I got carried away for a moment."

"Oh, so now you're apologizing?"

Gaspard reached for his wine glass, drank and swallowed hard. He then turned his attention back to Roger and said, "The point is that the Congolese couldn't rule their own country or form a single unified government. What little authority they had was that of local despots. The Portuguese might not know how to speak with a clear head, and they were slavers, but in the long run, they laid out the groundwork for freeing parts of Congo from under the yoke of unfit tyrants and brought about a semblance of peace and order. We're here to continue their work and to rectify their mistakes, to improve the natives' lives, and to protect them from what little slave trade remains from the Arabs."

"That was a magnificent short speech, one that sounds almost straight from King Leopold's mouth," Roger commented. "So far I've mostly been served words, and not real deeds."

"Whether or not you like it, Mr Casement, you are on the same boat with him and me. I'm positive that the more time you spend out here in the frontier, the more you'll come to agree with our methods to bring about the Western civilization to the natives."

Julienne returned to the room. Cécile diverted their attention to her by asking if something was wrong. Julienne looked down, shook her head and mumbled that the dessert was ready soon.

"Well, that's good news. I've grown bored of this interim," Cécile said. "There's some leftovers from the food, however. Perhaps we should set the rest aside for poor Henrik."

"A good idea," Gaspard noted before Cécile turned back to Julienne and said, "you can make yourself useful and take them to him."

Julienne lifted her eyes up a bit, but lowered them as soon as she had done so. She mumbled, "But…my lady…"

"Yes? What is it? Don't stutter."

"Who will finish preparing the dessert?"

"What a silly question. Alphonse is right there, is he not? He can do it. It can't be that hard."

Julienne passed her eyes to him, and offered a shy nod. Nsala offered an equally timid nod. Then they brought the silver plate and sauce bowl back to the kitchen. She moved the leftovers to a smaller plate, placed a dome over it, and left the room. Nsala stayed behind.

Following Julienne's instructions, he took out the ready pastry from the refrigerator and placed it on a table. The pastry looked odd: it consisted of three layers of dough with cream between them, while the top layer was covered with frosting, chocolate drizzle and sliced almonds. It looked unnecessarily complex. Wasn't food just something that you're meant to eat and not admire at?

He glanced at the recipe book to see what more needed to be done for the ornament piece. The book advised him to cut the pastry into smaller parts for serving. He only needed to measure their length to make sure the pieces would be evenly cut.

That was easier said than done. When he lifted the knife after cutting the last part in two, the outermost slice fell to its side and to the table. Nsala bit his teeth together and lifted the slice up with his fingers. The frosting hadn't had enough time to solidify, and some of it clung to his fingers, while splatters of cream smeared the table's surface.

It only now occurred to him that he should've used the knife to pick up the slice instead. That might've kept it representable enough and hid the accident, but it was too late for that. Anyone could see that he had touched the slice with his fingers.

Another thought passed by him: he could just eat the slice. It felt wrong somehow to tempt fate like that. The pastry wasn't meant for him, and yet, no-one would ever have to know about it. Better to hide the tracks and hope for the best.

Without giving it much more thought, he stuffed the entire slice into his mouth. He tried to be as quick as he could, but it was impossible to eat something like that without stopping to savour the taste. It was unlike anything he had ever tried. It was the best thing he had ever eaten, and before he realized it, it was gone from his mouth.

All that remained were the smears of cream on the table's surface. He glanced at them, swiped them off with his hand, and then put his fingers into his mouth to relive some sensation of that sweet taste. He had just swallowed them and wiped his hand against his weathered pants when Julienne returned.

"Good, you finished preparing the dessert. Now you should go back, in case they want something more."

"And you?"

"The fat crone wants some tea with her pastry, so I'll make some for her."

She didn't seem to notice the missing piece. Nsala left the kitchen and assumed his original position by the dining room's wall. He felt nervous all of a sudden, and let his eyes wander at the table's feet, following its gentle curves and polished umber surface. Gaspard, Cécile and Roger were all just waiting for the dessert in silence.

Julienne brought it not long after. She placed it on the table, bowed and said that she'd bring the tea next.

While Cécile admired the pastries, Roger asked her if they were the surprise she had mentioned earlier.

"They are. Thousand sheets, my favourite dessert," she said with a bright smile. "When I ordered the ingredients in Boma, I had no idea when I'd get to enjoy the food itself. I'm glad you happened to be here at this exact time."

"So am I. It's not every day that you get to eat something like this so far from Europe."

"You're right about that," she said with a smile and passed her eyes over the pastries again. "But looking at them, do they seem a bit off to you?"

"I don't know," Gaspard said and leaned in. "Do you see something out of the ordinary, Mr Casement?"

"None whatsoever. They seem perfectly fine to me."

"No, the pastries are placed more on the left side of the plate."

"Nonsense. It's just your eyes playing tricks," Gaspard dismissed.

"You two don't have any eye for spatial visualization, do you? The pastries are clearly placed several centimetres to the left."

Julienne returned with a tray that held a tea pot and three cups on it. While handing out the cups to each one, she noticed Cécile's stare at the corner of her eye.

"Is something wrong, my lady?" she managed to ask.

"It's like there's missing one pastry from the plate," Cécile demanded. "You wouldn't happen to know anything about it, would you?"

Julienne passed her eyes over the plate and looked like she wanted to say something, but Cécile was quick to take her initial stutters as assent.

"You thief! I'm sure my dessert was good change to whatever rotten food you usually eat with your dirty hands," she snapped, and then her eyes opened wide. "You also ate some of the mutton meant for poor Henrik, didn't you? I bet you did! How could you? Have you no shame? Stealing food from an ill young man!"

"Dear, calm down now," Gaspard intervened and stood up. "It's only one slice. There's no need for uncalled theatrics over such a small thing."

"Who knows how long this has been going on? She only got caught red-handed now because she couldn't resist touching my favourite food!"

"Who knows what happened to that one slice. Maybe it fell on the floor. You wouldn't want to eat something that has touched the floor, would you?"

"You make one concession like that, and suddenly you have mice jumping all over the table!" Cécile cried.

While she took turns scolding Julienne and lamenting on how the evening was now ruined, Nsala stood quietly by the wall. Roger shared in his uneasiness.

7. The Blind and the Timid

The next morning came quietly. The sun just barely peeked over the horizon when Roger stepped outside of his guest room, his usually well-cared hair in a tousle. The light-yellow spots marking the armpits on his shirt had turned more permanent with each day that had passed, and were now fully visible when he leaned over to light a smoking pipe with a match.

Henrik slept in the room next to his. A small plate with a dome over it had been left at his doorstep and gone untouched. John sniffed at it, but turned his head away. The dog left the spoiling meat for a swarm of flies that buzzed anxiously around it, looking for any opening to squeeze in and get a taste of yesterday's feast.

Roger shooed away an errant fly orbiting around his head with his pipe and turned his thoughts to yesterday. The dinner had gone nowhere near like he had imagined. The friendly-minded conversation over good food that he had envisioned had been thwarted first by Gaspard's staunch beliefs, and then by Cécile's outburst towards the end. Roger had eaten a slice of the dessert out of courtesy, and then headed straight to bed with his apologies. Sleep had come to him with surprising ease despite the whirlwind of thoughts in his head. It must've been thanks to the best meal he had had in almost three months.

But now those same thoughts of unfinished work came back to him, clearer than ever. There wasn't much more that he could get out of Gaspard, while Cécile seemed outright ignorant of anything and everything that took place outside the mansion's walls. And at this time, both must've still been sleeping off yesterday's tears and shock.

Lucas might've helped him with his work, then. He at least seemed like he wanted to help, but perhaps not too much. Not in a way that would intervene in the natural order of things around here. Henrik, in turn, was in no shape to talk to, that much was clear. And David, despite his command of French, seemed utterly unwilling to speak of anything else other than going over in detail the many and various benefits that imperialism had to offer.

Roger's mind turned to Nsala. Out of all the people who had passed his thoughts this morning, he was the one he hadn't had a good opportunity to speak with as of yet. Maybe he'd be up in the early morning like him. Finding him would perhaps give the satisfaction of completing yesterday's unfinished business.

He banged his pipe gently against a wooden support to get rid of the ashes in his pipe, and left it in his guestroom. Then he whistled at the dog to follow him. The caked mud cracked under his boots. He didn't have to walk long before coming across a hunched figure by a water pump.

"Good morning, Nsala," Roger greeted him. "I trust you slept well yesterday."

"Oh, Mr Casement, sir. I didn't see you there," the hunched man answered and stood up. He added after a short pause, "I didn't sleep very well yesterday, no."

"I understand. The dinner didn't exactly have a happy ending."

"It didn't, sir."

"I feel that I'm partly at blame."

"What do you mean, sir?" Nsala asked and his eyes widened.

"The whole sorry affair was my suggestion," Roger told. "I felt that I had more to discuss with Gaspard, but came to realize at the table that it wasn't true. He speaks a lot and keeps offering justification for the way he's doing things, but most of what he's saying is just empty air. Something that doesn't actually help me in my work."

"What do you plan to do, sir?"

"To really get an idea of this place, I need to speak with the locals. People like you. You can help me with that."

"Is that the reason you had me brought here, sir?"

"I do. And please, Nsala: you don't have to call me a 'sir'," Roger emphasized. "I've never liked it when others do that."

"I'll try," Nsala said, paused and swallowed the last word.

"Then, to answer your question, I'd hoped that you could help me with my work for a few weeks at most, and after that, return to Bomenga. But it seems that Gaspard would like to keep you around," Roger said. "Before anything else, I'd like to know how you feel about it."

"I'm not sure, to be honest. I think it's too early to say anything. Before yesterday, I had only seen Mr Bunschoten a couple of times and never spoken to him. He has always felt like a distant figure to me and everyone else."

"He told me as much. He said that he's been reluctant to show his face around because the last state official left things in a sorry state, and that restoring the bonds of trust would take time."

"That would be an understatement, sir."

"Yes. I saw that boy and the man without arms from the time of the rubber terror. The four men tied to the wood poles weren't much of an improvement, no matter what Gaspard claims."

Nsala shifted in place, as if just the thought of them made him uncomfortable. The gesture didn't miss Roger. He asked, "Were you here back in those times?"

"Back in the rubber terror?" Nsala asked, and Roger nodded. He continued, "No, something that I'm thankful for. I narrowly missed it."

"That's good to hear, but you also don't have any memory of the previous official?"

"No. I know nothing of him. And yesterday was the first time that I met Mr Bunschoten properly, if you can say that, as well as his wife. I didn't even know he had a wife."

"They both seem to keep to themselves. What were your impressions of her?"

Nsala hesitated for a moment, and then admitted that she didn't leave a good first impression.

"No, she did not. Although, when she had her bout, I would've expected Gaspard to stand by her side, no matter how ridiculous her reason was. Yet he didn't," Roger thought aloud. "He didn't express any concern or regret over tying people to poles and withholding them water, so I don't understand why he took Julienne's side in the matter. Would you know why?"

"I don't. I likewise met Julienne only yesterday."

"I see. Do you think she'd have something useful to add on what happened?"

"She might, but there's no need for you to ask her."

"Why not?"

"Because," Nsala began, "because I dropped that slice to the table. It became smeared, so I ate it so that no-one would find out."

"It was your doing?"

"Julienne didn't deserve the scolding," Nsala said hastily. Then he threw himself down on his knees and almost begged, "Forgive me, sir. I thought it'd be harmless. I feel horrible over what happened. I beg for your forgiveness, sir."

"You have nothing to forgive to me," Roger said slowly, "only to Julienne. She, however, might not be as understanding."

"You're not going to tell anyone?"

"No. What would it benefit? It would only cause…"

"Oh, thank you, sir! Thank you!"

"…more needless harm. What's done is done. However, I appreciate your sincerity in the matter. It makes me certain that you're the right person to help me in my work."

"Thank you one more time, sir," Nsala said with his hands together. He stood up and added, "Whatever you need help with, I'll help."

Roger nodded and said, "I mentioned that I'd like to look around this place, the mansion's surroundings and the plantations. I'd like for you to come with me."

"Of course. Just say when you planned to go?"

"I was thinking now."

"Now?"

"Is the timing a problem to you?"

"Well, I…I don't really know. It's only my second morning here," Nsala backtracked. "Gaspard and Cécile are still sleeping, so I think I can spare an hour of my time."

"Excellent."

"Just, before we go, help me carry the other water bucket to the kitchen. Julienne will be waiting for them to prepare breakfast."

"Of course," Roger said and picked up a bucket, "although I'm surprised Cécile allows her to keep working in the kitchen after yesterday."

"Julienne's the only one she has for that," Nsala said, pumped the other bucket full, and took it with him.

A low, indifferent voice greeted Nsala when he opened a door leading to the mansion's kitchen. Nsala answered something in the local tongue. When Roger walked inside, Julienne gave him a quick glance, looked away, and then her eyes bolted back at the unexpected visitor. She was chewing on something before that, and now swallowed hard, bowed down and apologized.

Nsala said something to her, and Roger forced a smile on his face despite not understanding the words.

"Alright. If you must go with him, then go," she said in French, stood up slowly and then returned to work with some hesitation. Roger noted a bruise on her gaunt cheek, and a small bowl that had in it what looked like dried leaves and strips of bark.

"What was she eating?" Roger asked once they had walked some distance from the door. "Some sort of medicine for the bruise?"

"I don't think so. She ate the same thing yesterday morning. Maybe she just likes it? I don't know, to be honest."

Roger gave his words a nod and switched topic, "I also picked up that she called you by your real name, but you didn't call her Julienne. I take it that's not her real name any more than Alphonse is yours."

"Her name's Ilanga. She told me Gaspard gave her the other name because he thinks it's a pretty one."

"I see. And Father Lucas was the one who gave you your other name."

"Yes," Nsala answered and noted Roger's wrinkled brow.

"You seem a bit surprised by these names. Why?"

"Not surprised, but a bit amused. It's not nearly as common in the other parts of Africa where I've been assigned to work before," Roger told. "I have a servant in Boma, a young man that I saved from an officer of the Force Publique when he was just a boy. He never gave me his real name, so I named him Charlie. He has always been more of an exception in that regard."

"Lucas told me that you're from a different country and have a different king. But that is something that I don't understand," Nsala brought up. "Are you from another part of Belgium than Gaspard and Lucas? Do you belong to a different tribe than them?"

Roger gave his words a short laugh mixed in with a huff, "I'm actually not Belgian at all."

"Not at all?"

"No."

"But you're from Europe, right?"

"I am, but not from Belgium."

"Belgium and Europe are not the same?"

"They are not," Roger said and extended his arm forward. "Walk with me, and I'll explain."

Roger told him how the nations of Europe could be likened to the disparate tribes and petty kingdoms of Congo, and how most were ruled by monarchs. He told Nsala how he was from one such nation, Ireland, and had been sent to Congo on behalf of a completely different nation, The Great Britain.

"And that's the reason why you don't fear King Leopold?" Nsala asked as they arrived by some straw huts.

"Yes. He is not my king, and I'm not here to represent him. Leopold is in fact quite hated in Europe because of everything that has been reported about Congo," Roger explained.

"And to make sense of those reports, you need my help?"

"For that exact reason," Roger said with a nod. "I hope that clears the situation to you."

"It does. I've felt that Lucas wants to help, like you, but he has been afraid of King Leopold all this time. That has made him stay his hand."

"That was my exact impression of him as well."

"He has never done anything as brave as you have," Nsala said. "I'm not a brave man."

"You are."

"I'm simply doing my job."

"But unlike the other Europeans, you're doing something that nobody else is."

Roger kept quiet this time. He looked him in the eyes for a few seconds before turning them away. Then they moved on. Roger wished to walk through the plantations with Nsala. It weren't really the inconspicuous coffee or cacao beans that he was interested in, but the smaller patches of rubber trees that could be found farther away from the shore.

"Gaspard told me that no wild India-rubber is collected around the lake anymore," Roger mentioned when they walked past the first trees. His hand reached for the small notebook and pen tucked in the right pocket of his pants.

"Not anymore, no."

"And that its collection was replaced by the cultivated rubber trees later on to keep up with the demand back in Europe."

"As you can see."

"How exactly is the rubber extracted from the planted trees? How does it differ from the India-rubber?"

"Well, the wild rubber, this India-rubber as you call it, is a liana that climbs up trees all the way to the canopy. You use a knife to make slices to the stem and then pour out the rubber. To get all of it from a single liana, you'd either have to climb up the tree to make several cuts, or just pull the whole plant down to the ground," Nsala explained. "But with the cultivated trees, you only need to slice the trunk and let the rubber pour out slowly."

"That sounds much easier," Roger said in between the pen's scribbling sounds.

"It is, but it still takes a considerable amount of work," Nsala said and pointed to a man with an iron bucket. At first glance, he didn't appear out of the ordinary. Perhaps he held his arms awkwardly apart from his body, and walked much like someone who had spent too much time on a horse's saddle. But after squinting his eyes, Roger could see that parts of his arms, chest and thighs were covered under layers of almost transparent, gelatinous goo.

"When you pour out the rubber, you have to place it onto your body so that it doesn't solidify," Nsala said. "Then you have to scrape it off later. It's…painful, at first, but then not so much."

"How come?"

"The rubber takes all of your body hair with it."

"You seem to know a lot about this topic. Do you have experience in it?"

Nsala spelled out the next words more slowly, "I used to collect rubber before, but only from the cultivated trees. I heard of the old methods from others. Most aren't around anymore."

"And when we met, you were Lucas' aide."

Nsala hesitated again before saying, "Lucas taught us French most days between work. I picked up the language faster than others."

"What motivated you to do so?"

"I don't really know. Perhaps it's just something I did out of boredom? Working with the rubber trees is slow and takes patience, so I had time to practice the language with my own thoughts. Speaking it out loud to myself, conjugating the verbs in my mind. Or maybe I just thought that learning it could be useful one day."

"I think it was. Otherwise you wouldn't be here telling me all about it."

"I guess."

"You said I was a brave man, but I'm only here to take notes and then leave," Roger said as they walked away. "But for you, Nsala, this is your home. You're braver than me for telling me all of this."

They continued on to the small village near the mansion. There was a warehouse that was more of a shallow, large roof over flat ground. Under it were some early bundles of sacks that had already been piled up there after yesterday. Two soldiers looked after them.

"I think it's actually odd that I began my work at Bomenga."

"How come?"

"Bomenga is some distance away from the mansion, but Bikoro is right here next to it."

"Bikoro is much smaller than Bomenga. This village was here before the Belgians arrived, but most of it was levelled during the rubber terror to make room for the Belgians' needs, and to house their soldiers," Nsala explained. "Most who lived here were forced to move to Bomenga. And when Gaspard took over and the rubber terror ended, those who had moved to Bomenga chose to stay there instead of moving back, as they had built new homes for themselves."

"You said earlier that you narrowly missed the rubber terror."

"I did."

"Then I take it that you're not from either one of these villages?"

"I'm not. I'm from a village north-east of here. Most of who work for Gaspard nowadays are from such surrounding villages."

"Because so many of the original villagers have died…"

Nsala gave his realization a slow nod. Roger underlined some of his notes before turning his eyes at the uniform sacks.

He tried to guess their contents, and estimate their weight. Someone came by and dropped a heavy sack on the ground. He stood up, saw the white man staring at him and straightened his back before walking away with a quick pace.

"Would you be willing to tell me about how you avoided the terror? Of course, only if you're comfortable with the subject."

Nsala took a moment to search his memory for the right words to say, and then uttered slowly, "I had my first child just before the rubber terror began. A daughter. A short time before the Belgians arrived. They took most of the men with them, but made a rare exception for me because of the little toddler clutching my chest. Then, some five years later, I think, just when the terror had ended, I came here because the child was old enough."

"Did you had to come here?"

Nsala stayed quiet this time. Roger studied his face and then continued, "Gaspard told me that you're not really employees here, but instead doing something of a public service to the Free State. Is that how you'd describe it?"

"I don't know what an employee is, only that the Belgians expect work from us. It's not any different from what I was used to," Nsala said. "Someone in power expects something from you, and you do that. It doesn't matter if that person is a chieftain or a foreign king."

"What about the mother?"

"What about her?"

"Is she looking after your child while you're here?"

"No," Nsala admitted. "She…she died giving birth. But that's something I don't want to talk about. Please."

"Of course."

"I know however that my daughter is safe with people I know, although I haven't seen her in a long time. She helps the others at the village farms."

"She has to work? Why?" Roger asked. "Can't you send her money or food?"

"Not really," Nsala said and looked around. "The pay I receive isn't much, barely enough to get by. Gaspard demands that all the villages around the lake provide him either labour here at the plantations, or food at their respective villages. Every man, woman, child and elderly person has to work."

"I had no idea. And the punishment for being uncooperative is to end up chained to a pole."

"Mr Casement, a surprise to see you up so early," a familiar voice greeted them from behind and cut short whatever Nsala wanted to say in return.

The newcomer turned out to be David, dressed in the same spotless blue uniform and red cap that made him stand out from the others around him. He had a bundle of dried leaves in his hands.

Roger put away his notebook and pen and returned him the greeting. Nsala muttered in a low voice after him, "Good morning, Officer Fidèle."

David passed his eyes over Nsala and chewed his tongue a couple of times. He then turned his attention to Roger and asked, "Mr Casement, what are you doing here at this time?"

"My work, the same as you, I reckon."

"I think our jobs are very different," David gave his words a friendly laugh and kneeled down to pat the bulldog John on the head. "Speaking of that, I heard Gaspard held a fancy dinner party for you yesterday evening."

"He did."

"Sadly, I wasn't invited. I think it was for whites only?"

"It was," Roger said with a low voice.

"I understand. Was Henrik there?"

"At first, but he was too tired to stay for long. Whatever got into him before our visit to Bomenga forced him back to bed soon enough."

"That's a shame," David said, and his tense shoulders fell down. "How was he doing? Otherwise, I mean."

"He kept quiet and slouching in his chair. Most of what he said were indifferent murmurs and profanities."

"Hah, that sounds like him. It's good to know he at least still has his sense of humour."

"Well, that's one way to look at it. The Bunschotens weren't as amused by them," Roger said. "Henrik didn't miss out on much, though. The food was good, excellent even given the circumstances, but Gaspard's wife had a fit towards the end. I ended up leaving early because of it."

"A shame, shame, indeed. I'm sorry for you and Henrik that the dinner went like that," David said, peeled back some of the leaves and took a bite of the food inside. "If you're hungry, you should get one of these."

"What is it?"

"It's fresh kwanga, ah, cassava bread. It's good."

"They sell bread here?"

"They do," David said and motioned towards a small building behind him. It stood out from the others around it by being larger and built out of sparsely set planks. A sign by the door confirmed the place as a 'convenience store'.

"You know, we never had anything like these before you Europeans came to Africa."

"You mean convenience stores?" Roger asked.

"Yes. They're so handy. Just the thought of being able to buy food or anything else you need at most hours was unimaginable to us only a decade ago."

"It can't be that different from local markets."

"Well, we had those, on certain days, and you could always barter something from a neighbour, but they weren't as…convenient, as these," David said with a smile that tried to hide in it the slight embarrassment he felt over his choice of word.

"Maybe you should visit the stores in Europe one day. The one in Bikoro looks like nothing compared to the ones in Europe."

"I believe you, Mr Casement. Everything that I've heard of Europe makes it sound like the most magnificent place on earth. And everything that has ever come out of there confirms those stories to be true," David said and let his imagination run for a moment. "In the meanwhile, if you're hungry, you should get some fresh kwanga. Think of it as experiencing a part of our culture as well. You know, one of the only good parts."

"I'll think on it."

"Well, Mr Casement, I'll be seeing you around," David said. "It was good meeting you like this, but now I have to get back on patrol."

Roger said his farewells, and Nsala muttered the same. When David was gone, Roger asked Nsala why he had turned so quiet all of a sudden.

"I didn't want to speak over the officer, or without being asked something."

"Were you afraid of him?"

"No, not really," Nsala hesitated. "It's more that most of the soldiers simply think too highly of themselves, that they've been given special positions by the Belgians, and they don't like it when their expectations aren't met."

"I see," Roger said and wrung his brow. "I got the impression that you had something you wanted to say before David surprised us. What was it?"

Nsala looked away with an open mouth, and after a short moment shook his head. He said, "I don't remember what it was."

"Are you sure it wasn't anything important? It was about your daughter."

"I'm sure I'd remember something like that. I also think that I've already taken enough of your time, sir, and that I should return to the mansion to help Ilanga with her morning chores."

"Of course," Roger said in a low voice, "but before you go, I'd like to ask something else."

"I'm not in a rush. What is it?"

"I'd like to see these villages around the lake that you mentioned. I think they'd offer invaluable perspective to my work. Would you be willing to accompany me on these short voyages?"

"I don't think you understand just how large Lake Mantumba is, sir, or how deep in the jungle most of the villages are. It would take you months to visit all of them. It takes almost a week's worth of travelling by foot just to get to my home village from here," Nsala said.

Roger nodded his head in acknowledgement, and said, "Then, if I'd just visit the coastal villages, could you come with me? I have my own boat, with a steam engine and all."

"That's doable, but it will still take you at least half a day just to get to most of those villages. I'm sorry, sir, but I simply cannot leave my new duties here for entire days, unless Gaspard gives his approval to it."

"I'm certain he won't. He has taken a liking to you."

"You could ask Father Lucas," Nsala suggested. "He is fluent in Bangi, my native tongue. It's the language that is spoken around the entire lake."

Roger pondered his suggestion for a moment, and then agreed to it. He doubted there was little more he could learn from Lucas, but at least having him by his side would make conversing with the locals possible. At some point, he'd have to leave and get back to the coast and the telegraph office there. And judging from the urgency of the request he had received two months ago, the men in power back home would want the report sooner rather than later.

8. The Estranged

Nsala balanced a heavy tray over his arms. On it were two cups and a tea pan, the same one that he had become intimately familiar with during the past week and a half. It was wide and flat, made of bronze, and had two snakes running across the lid. Or at least they looked like snakes to him, roaring snakes with fur, stubby legs and claws.

The tea pan didn't look like European to him, or at least like anything else in the house. It looked like it came from somewhere else altogether. Not from Congo, that much was clear, but from somewhere else. Lucas had passingly mentioned to him that such places existed, but Nsala couldn't remember any by name. And he couldn't even begin to guess what those places were like, what the people there looked like, or what they sounded like. He only knew that those other places had also been subjugated by the same foreigners from the sea.

He brought the tray outside to the mansion's terrace, where he found Gaspard and Cécile in the middle of a discussion.

"…and be sure to get me a copy of every newspaper that has arrived from Europe when you board that steamer to Boma tomorrow evening."

"I know, I know, Gaspard. I must've done this a hundred times by now."

"It's the only use that comes out of your excursions."

"Well, maybe to you, but remember that I never wanted to be dragged to this sorry place." Nsala placed the tray to a small wicker table. It bent a bit under the tray's weight.

"A woman's place should be by her husband's side, no matter where that takes her."

"You're thinking too much of your career. What has Leopold ever done to you that has earned him your love over mine?"

"You're my wife, Cécile. You know I'll always love you, and have done so from the moment we met, but men also have a duty to their country," Gaspard said, but the words didn't come off with the same natural confidence that his voice was usually so full of. "The world needs ambitious people like Leopold who are brave enough to push the boundaries. If it wasn't for his vision, Belgium would still be a small country for small people, and we'd be nothing more than two vintners living somewhere by the border with the Netherlands and mumbling Dutch to each other."

Cécile said something in a language that sounded unlike French. Nsala didn't understand a word of it.

"Whatever that means," Gaspard said with a sigh. "You know it I don't like it when you speak Dutch. It's a crude language only fit for peasants."

"I said I'd actually prefer living in the countryside near the border with the Netherlands."

Nsala poured tea to their cups. Gaspard thanked him passingly, and continued, "Anyway, I need to know what the press are saying of our country and Leopold back home."

"Reading those newspapers always makes you so angry."

"Of course it does, with the amount of lies they're filled with," Gaspard said. "The British alone have let millions of Indians starve to death because they made the natives cultivate cotton instead of rice, and nobody in Europe has batted an eye. Yet when it comes to Congo, everyone has a problem with a few exaggerated accounts by some missionaries, and mostly American Protestant ones at that. And that's all the reason the British needed to send Casement here to bother us, like they have some God-given right to stick their noses into everyone else's business."

"Be as it may, you must know it's a lost battle already."

"It's not. Leopold is doing everything he can to expose their hypocrisy."

"From what I've heard in Boma, most people hate Leopold. I don't think that Roger's work will matter that much in the long run, as people have already made up their mind on the matter. Leopold will lose, sooner or later."

"You're right to say that the people's opinion is the only thing that matters, and I need to stay on top of those developments back home."

"To find more arguments against Roger? And the person who will come after him? Something that will help you shape the truth?" Cécile asked, but more to herself. Then she added with a sigh, "He's going to leave soon. Roger, I mean."

"Thankfully. He's spent the last week and a half cruising around the lake and sniffing at its every foetid corner. I don't really see what he's been after this whole time."

"What do you think is going to be on that report of his?"

"Not much, I'm sure. When he gets back to London with empty hands, a lot of people are going to change their minds and understand they've been lied to. They're going to come crawling back to Leopold and apologize for insulting his humanitarian views, and Leopold will have me to thank for that."

She let Gaspard bask in the glory that he had imagined for himself before saying, "Roger's work doesn't matter in the grand picture. Leopold will lose. No one likes him. We might as well pack our things and head."

Gaspard slammed his fist on his chair's armrest, picked up the other cup and slurped the tea. The hard wicker weave had left its mark on the underside of his fist, and the hot tea turned his cheeks red.

"Just get me those damn newspapers."

Nsala had assumed a familiar downward looking position behind them, by the mansion's wall. It left him just out of the sun's rays that crept under the roof and onto the terrace. The sun rarely shone past the perpetual grey mattress of clouds that covered the sky, so the rare sunshine had been reason enough for Gaspard and Cécile to have their usual morning tea outside instead of the living room.

Cécile waited for a moment to pick up her cup of tea, blew on it gently, and sipped some of its contents. Then she glanced at her husband and affirmed, "I'll get those newspapers for you."

"Good," Gaspard sighed and sank back into the pillows.

"But...shouldn't you at least be quiet about these things near Alphonse?"

"Why?"

"He can actually understand us, unlike Julienne."

"He's just a servant. It doesn't matter if he hears us," Gaspard said and kept his eyes on the floor. "And besides, if you're that afraid of him, then that's just one more reason to keep Julienne around."

"Afraid of him? No. He's a much better servant than Julienne has ever been. But he could tell Roger what we've discussed over the past days."

"Why do you think I've kept him so close to me all this time?" he asked. "It was a mistake to agree to Casement's suggestion so soon. I should've instead waited for him to leave before taking on Alphonse, but at least this way he can't speak to Casement behind my back."

"Well, it's good that you've already thought of it," she said, "but it also begs another question. Why are you still keeping Julienne around?"

"She is a better chef."

"Alphonse can also cook."

"Not as well as she."

"He could improve."

"Maybe, but that would take time. In the meanwhile, you'd just miss how tasteless cassava can actually be."

Cécile huffed, and Gaspard continued, "Besides, the pay is so little that I might as well keep ten more servants around."

"Well, then all the more reason to fire that incompetent monkey. Or have you forgotten that she was caught eating our food?"

"You keep claiming that, but what proof do you have?"

"I don't need any proof for that! It's just…just…a woman's intuition, that's all," she stuttered and became frustrated. "I know she's been eating our food behind our backs."

"Just like it's your intuition that all of my work here is going down the gutter," he dismissed. "Julienne has been here for almost five years, almost as long as you and I. She's never done anything like that before, and I don't have a reason to suspect that she would've started now."

"I don't understand why you keep defending her."

"And I don't understand your insistence on blaming her. You should just trust your husband, and not worry your head too much with it."

"Or maybe, for at least once, you should listen to what your wife has to say."

"I'm here to represent the Free State," Gaspard said and placed his right hand's fingers over his chest. "If I did things your way, it would shake the natives' trust in our government."

"You say that while you treat your workers poorly."

"And how exactly have I treated them wrong?"

"You've chained people to wooden stakes. It's what Roger told me."

"There's nothing wrong with that. And for a consul, you'd think that Casement would have a better grasp at how laws work."

"Roger was right when he said that there's no need to have two servants when one can do all the needed work. Alphonse should be able to do everything that Julienne has done, and more even, given that he actually has some muscle to him."

Their argument started to go in a circle again. So far in the past week and a half, the husband and wife hadn't spent that much time together, but when they had, their conversations about the cloudy weather, the hot tea and shared liking towards the mansion's new servant almost always devolved into quarrels that led nowhere and ended in an uneasy silence. Cécile would start complaining that there was nothing to do, that the food was bad, that Julienne should be thrown out, that they should head back home that Roger was leaving soon, that Gaspard didn't appreciate her paintings, and that the steamer to Boma wouldn't arrive soon enough. Nsala had already heard it all in a week and a half, and memorized the litany out of boredom. Gaspard, in turn, contented himself with complaining about his wife's complaining.

A shift in Gaspard's tone woke him from his stupor.

"...your own fascination with the same consul. Don't think I haven't noticed it."

"What? That's just absurd, Gaspard. I'd never even think of something like that."

"Nonsense. Before Casement you had an eye on Henrik."

"It's nothing like that."

"Then what was it?"

"He's only a young boy. He must miss Europe terribly, the same as I do, but he can't leave this hellhole to visit Boma. It's only fair that someone looks after him, like a mother would. Or no, not like a mother, but more like an aunt," she blurted out and added. "My God, Henrik's not even half my age!"

"Ah, but Casement is about the same age, isn't he? Yet he has never mentioned having a wife. It makes one wonder if everything's right by him."

"You mean down below?"

"No, I mean up in his head."

"Oh, no, no, that can't be it," she uttered and shook her head.

"It could also explain why he's stuck in his career as a mere consul. Most people of his age working for a foreign service are already ambassadors," Gaspard continued, certain that he was right. "Nobody likes a sinner."

"I don't think it's that."

"Then what else would it be? His rash behaviour unfit of a man working for a foreign service? That he's Irish, essentially a second class citizen in his own country? Or come to think of it, perhaps it's all three of them? He's a boorish, homosexual Irishman. Hardly an ideal man to represent any government."

She shook her head and reasoned. "Most people in Boma live by themselves. They don't have wives or children, or if they do, they aren't with them in Congo. I think the reason Roger doesn't have a wife is because he, like the rest of the foreign delegates, is simply someone who understands that the kind of life he wants for himself isn't for having a family, and that others shouldn't have to suffer for."

"You're insufferable."

"Well, give it some more thought, Gaspard: we could be the same unhappy couple that we're now, but instead live comfortably in the Belgian countryside."

"Why not just leave back to Belgium then?"

This time Cécile didn't have any answer ready. She took some of her tea to buy time to think, but Gaspard was quicker.

"You couldn't leave, could you, because part of you agrees with me? A part that understands that we're here for a reason, and in time, will be rewarded for that," Gaspard said and motioned towards the guest houses. "It's the same reason why Casement is here. He believes that he, too, will be rewarded for everything that he's doing here. And the same is true for Henrik as well, no matter how much he agrees with you on this place."

Nsala noticed a smile creeping over Gaspard's face. He knew he had won their daily argument, like on most days, and let the conversation slip elsewhere.

"That reminds me that we haven't really checked in on Henrik lately, have we?" Cécile asked.

"No, we haven't."

"Should we check in on him? I think we should check in on him."

"For once, I agree."

"We should also give him some quinine and fresh bed sheets for his malaria."

"I suppose we can, but they haven't worked before. I'm still not sure what went into him."

He turned around in his chair and asked Nsala to go and knock on the guest room's door. Nsala did what he was asked, but heard no response from the other side. He knocked again, this time with a bit more force, while the couple watched on from the terrace. He heard no response on the second time either, but caught a whiff of something. Something that didn't smell right, and made him blow air out of his nostrils to get rid of it. He then returned to Gaspard.

"Well, what's the matter?"

"Henrik didn't respond, sir. And I caught a smell of something musty."

"He hasn't left his room in, what, two days now? Young men sweat so much. The whole room must be drenched in it by now. We should definitely change the bed sheets."

Gaspard teetered on the edge of his chair and rubbed his chin. Then he got up and said, "This doesn't feel right. I'll go have a look myself."

"Henrik must be asleep. It's still morning. We shouldn't disturb the poor boy."

Gaspard walked past her and onto the wet mud. Nsala followed him. Gaspard banged on the door, and when he didn't hear a response, he kicked in the door.

9. Minor Noble's Grand Adventure

It would've been easy to think that after spending a week and a half crisscrossing Lake Mantumba daily one would become accustomed to its stillness, but Roger hadn't. The entire place felt unnatural, dead: almost as if whatever life still resided in the waters had been struck by the stagnant heat and left at the bottom to rot. There were no fish or birds underneath the clouded sky, only the marvel of modern technology that intruded upon its peace with the steady beat of a steam engine.

"How many villages has it already been?" Lucas asked. "I've lost count."

"Ten," Roger answered, lowered the binoculars and looked over his shoulder. "One for every day. And this one will be the eleventh, then."

"The last one."

"Well, eleven should be enough. It makes for a good sample size."

"I hope so, although it's not every village around the lake."

"You can stay for longer, if you wish," Lucas said. "You don't have to leave us just yet."

He sat on the small steamer's deck sideways, one eye staring into nothingness and leaning in on his cane. Roger stood in front of him, one hand taking support from the boat's makeshift roof, and the other holding the pair of binoculars. His eyes had returned to the distant, muddy shores, and the dark trees that curved over them.

"Maybe we could visit some of the villages inland next?" Lucas asked. "All this sitting on a boat hasn't done me any good. Even a little swing here and there makes me sick in the head."

"Do you think that traipsing all over a jungle would be more comfortable?"

Lucas gave his words a dry laugh, "I guess not. I'd just end up with a face full of mud every hour or so."

Roger huffed a bit of air out of his nose. It was his way to share in the laughter. Then he said, "I was thinking of the same at first, I mean, to visit the villages inland. But as vast as the lake and its surroundings feel, Mantumba is only one small part of Congo. Some of the reports that I came here to investigate originate from further upstream. It's there that I must go next. And as much as I hate to say it, I feel like I've already wasted a good deal of time around here."

"How come?"

"Everything I've seen over the past week and a half has made me more and more assured that Gaspard and the Free State are actually trying to turn things around. Slowly maybe, very slowly, but the direction is right. And often the most consistent way to bring about change is to do it slowly," Roger told. "I hope that the visit to this last village won't change things."

"Then how have you wasted your time?"

"Another half-empty village recovering from the time of the rubber terror wouldn't add anything new to my work. And if something worse is taking place elsewhere in Congo, then it's either going to end up out of my report, or persist for one day longer."

"I see your point," Lucas said with a nod. "I may not know that much about the history of this place, but if Mantumba was one of the worst affected areas five years ago, I think that gives a good picture as to how the other parts of Congo fare today."

"I hope you're right."

The boat came around a small peninsula. Lucas recalled a village around this part of the lake. His memory still served him well, and he could make enough from the blur he saw to tell that this was the right place. Behind the trees cloaked in beards of moss opened a clearing by the coast, a stretch of brown marked by dots of beige. Stacks of grey smoke rose from some of them.

Roger peered at the stretch of colour through his binoculars. He saw dozens of people clambering out of their huts and gathering by the shore. They looked at him, or at least his general direction, and motioned their arms around. Then one of them turned around all of a sudden. Others followed, and before they all had had time to turn around, a faint shout carried over the still water and the engine's purring. It was followed by others as the tiny specks scattered and scurried away.

One crewmember, a local man, shouted back at the village, but his reassurances rang to deaf ears. The distance and the panic by the shore drowned his futile efforts.

"It's the same thing every time, isn't it?" Roger asked without turning around. "Unfortunately. But they'll come back once they understand who we are."

"Let's hope so. I wouldn't want a repeat of yesterday when the locals wouldn't believe you, and just waited behind the tree line for us to leave."

"You can't blame them for their hesitation."

"No," Roger said, lowered his binoculars and shook his head. "It takes years to build trust, but only a moment to break it. And the Belgians had years to break it."

It took them a while to reach the shore and for the steamer to come to a stop near the empty shore. Two crewmembers jumped into the shallow water with bundles of rope in their arms and pulled the boat ashore. Roger helped Lucas find his footing on the wet mud, and John leaped after them. They approached the village together, Roger first with his hands out in the open and the bulldog by his side, and Lucas trudging behind.

The village had been almost completely abandoned on a moment's notice. The only ones who had stayed behind had done so involuntarily. Few individuals slouched against walls or on the ground, too delirious from sickness to understand what had even happened. One of them mumbled to the empty air in front of her. A baby's cry rang from somewhere. A fire burned in an open fireplace and a whiff of fresh food lingered in the air.

Perhaps the most striking feature about the village was that everything in it appeared new, from the huts to the tools that had been left behind, yet at the same time bleak and unrefined. There was no room for artistic expression. It wasn't the first such village either. The past week and a half had taught Roger that almost everyone who had lived around the lake at the time of the rubber terror had abandoned their homes and fled deep into the jungle, desperate to hide from the soldiers donning the bright blue uniforms and muzzle-loaded rifles. The ones that had lived through it all had only recently returned to their former homes and built everything from ground up. They were still hesitant of the dark stacks of smoke that at times cruised over the lake's surface, and of the pale spirits that travelled under them.

That same uneasiness could be felt in the air right now as well. Roger didn't see them, but he felt dozens of eyes staring at him from the tree line. They followed and judged his every move, but remained just as silent as the trees around them.

Roger came to a halt and turned to Lucas. He nodded, cleared his throat and began speaking. His feeble voice didn't carry far, and the jungle didn't answer.

"That could've gone better."

"What did you say?" Roger asked. "The usual?"

"The same. That we're unarmed missionaries visiting the village to see how the locals are doing."

"Let's see if the gift we brought with us would entice them to come meet us."

Lucas nodded and said, "A sack of dried cassava is the quickest way to earn a starving man's trust."

Roger made his way back to the steamer. A crewmember, a local man, offered to carry the sack for him, but Roger refused, reasoning it would be wiser to bring the gift to the villagers himself. They would've likely never seen a white man do a black one's work.

"Alright, let's try this again," Roger said, put the heavy sack down on the ground with a grunt, and loosened the robes around its mouth to reveal the contents inside.

Lucas hollered at the trees a second time, but the outcome ended up the same. The trees remained as silent as they had been before. Maybe even more so.

Roger saw movement in the corner of his eye. It was followed by a snap that had in it anger mixed in with fear. Then everything was silent again for a moment.

Something came out of the jungle. A thin skeleton with an arched back. It shouted something at Lucas, who hollered his answer to it. It asked another question. Lucas took few steps forward with the help of his cane, and the skeleton froze in place. Realizing his mistake Lucas stopped and gave a lengthier answer.

The skeleton remained silent for a while, no doubt judging what it had just seen and heard. Then it looked back at the jungle, and motioned towards the man. Other dark shadows of starvation crawled out of the jungle and into the light.

Lucas didn't lift his good eye from the emerging shapes, and whispered to the empty air in front of him without turning around.

"The locals ran because they thought we were with the Free State."

"That was obvious," Roger noted. "There doesn't appear to be many of them either, just like in the other villages."

The two backed away from the sack. The first local, the same skeleton, who dared close enough to the sack glanced at them, kneeled down and then glanced at them again. Then he thrust his hand inside and pulled out a fistful of brownish white roots.

His eyes opened wide, and he yelled something, a single word if Roger's ears were correct. He stood up and presented the treasure to the others, who at the sight of it rushed to the sack. Soon it disappeared into the middle of anxious feet, as the locals took turns to share the bounty among themselves and glance at the two strangers with unsure thanks and hesitation.

Someone approached from among the crowd. An older man whose age showed only in the wrinkles on his face, the bags under his eyes, and in what little tufts of white hair remained over his ears. His eyes met Roger's at the same level. He was followed by three women, all much younger than him.

The old man spoke something to him. Roger could only apologize in the native language, that he hadn't understood what the man had just said, and motioned towards Lucas. The old man glanced at Lucas, then returned Roger a puzzled look, as if insulted that he should speak with a cripple.

He spoke to him again, but Roger could only return him a careful smile. Lucas confirmed to Roger his assumptions about the man's hesitation.

"He's the chief of the village, and only agrees to speak to his equal. That means you. He takes you to be the senior missionary between us two."

"That's new. The others in the previous villages didn't have any reservations about speaking with you," Roger pondered. "Can you explain to the chief that you're my translator?"

Lucas did just that. At first, the chief nudged at the cripple's audacity, but then returned an unhappy murmur as a sign of agreement. He asked something. His words were still directed at Roger, but meant for Lucas now.

"The chief asks why you don't speak their language if we're both missionaries."

It had been a fairly common question in the past week and a half. Roger told that he had recently been transferred to Congo from another part of Africa, one where he had gotten by with French, and that he hadn't had time to learn the local language just yet. Lucas transferred the message to the chief.

The chief pondered the response, and then spoke for longer. He paused at times to give Lucas time to relay his message. He thanked for the food, and proceeded to say that if they had plans to gather people from his village and take them with them to learn about their nailed god, he wouldn't allow any to leave.

Roger asked why. The chief told that he needed every last one to work here.

Work on what, Roger asked. Work in the fields around the village, and to fish by the shore, the chief told.

Roger asked why he needed everyone in the village to work, and did that include children and elderly as well. The chief emphasized that everyone in the village worked to provide food for the white devil who inhabited the lake's other end.

Roger said that he had heard of this devil, this Gaspard, and would like to know what the chief thought of him. One of the women behind the chief shuddered when Roger said the word: she didn't need a translation to understand that particular hated word.

The chief told how they had only recently returned here, after years spent hiding elsewhere. Few trusted the devil's words that things would change, and even fewer trusted the brutes who had turned their backs on their kin and now worked for the devil. If they'd build better houses and fields by the shore, they'd very likely end up sacked and razed, like they had seven years ago. Only time would tell if the devil's promises had even an ounce of truth to them.

An idea occurred to Roger. Their visits to the other villages around the lake had yielded similar responses from others. Nsala had also told how the villages around the lake were under obligations to bring in a regular quota of food for the few whites and the small garrison of soldiers that remained in Bikoro. It was something that Gaspard had also mentioned, albeit indifferently and without much thought to it. Yet the quotas were something that most villages only barely managed to deliver.

Roger pointed behind the chief's back, at a small enclosure holding a few dozen fowls, and offered to buy ten of them. He expected a straight refusal, and it was exactly what he got from the chief. Even when Roger offered ten times the money Gaspard would ever pay for one and explained that the fowls would be used to prepare a communal meal for locals who had come to learn about their god's words, the chief still refused without giving the proposal a second thought.

His reasoning was simple: there was already little food left, the surrounding area produced less and less every month, and they didn't have energy or time to clear more forest for farmland or make more canoes for fishing. They could only hope to outlast whatever interests the foreigners had on the lake, and they couldn't eat the worthless brass rods that the missionaries offered.

Roger had begun to have a nagging feeling of regret for having enjoyed the meal Gaspard had served in his honour. The mutton had been excellent, in fact the best thing he had eaten the whole summer, but he still wasn't sure where the lamb had been from. Gaspard had claimed the lamb to be one of his own, but it could've just as likely been from one of the unfortunate villages around the lake. Stolen from the locals. If that were the case, he would've never even touched the cutlet in the first place. And yet again, he couldn't be sure of it.

Then, the chief offered further reasoning for his refusal: he didn't wish to get to know the whip any better, nor did anyone else in the village.

Roger turned to Lucas and asked, "A whip? Are you sure you translated that last part correctly?"

"That's what he said," Lucas confirmed. "A whip used to lash the locals."

"They're still using them? Why am I only learning of it now?"

"It doesn't happen often. It's the most severe punishment Gaspard has in store, and in your time here, no one has received any lashes. The last time, I think, was in mid-June."

"That doesn't excuse its continued use."

"I agree, and have brought it up with Gaspard, but he hasn't listened to me," Lucas said. "Perhaps you'd have better luck?"

"What's the use?" Roger dismissed. "He'd only come up with reasons to justify its use."

"That's exactly what he did with me. And if he hasn't told to you about it before, I don't see any other reason for it other than that he's been hiding it from you."

The chief had grown somewhat uneasy at their conversation. Behind him the others had emptied the sack's contents and dispersed around the village. Most had chosen to stick around and follow the conversation from a safe distance away.

The sudden uneasiness didn't slip by Lucas who said something to the chief.

The old man let out a laugh of disbelief. It wasn't a cruel laugh, more like how a parent would gently laugh at their child's innocent, naïve question. Then he spoke.

"I told him of your surprise that the locals have been punished with a lash. He said that he believes you now when you said that you're new around here," Lucas explained. "Everyone knows that the white devil punishes those who fail to meet his quotas."

The chief continued without waiting to hear the next question. He asked for several people to come forward from the crowd and show the entrant missionary what he meant.

Roger counted six people in total. The simple loincloths hanging from their waists left the scars on their thighs fully visible. Most were intricate webs of elevated skin. At parts the scars formed bulbous pockets that looked like they'd pop and begin to bleed if they'd be poked with a needle. All of the scars looked old as well. They were ample proof to back the chief's words. Roger made a note of them in his notebook.

"What makes this village different from the others?" he asked. "Why have the people been punished more than in the other ones?"

The chief was more hesitant to speak this time. He began slowly, as if admitting something deeply shameful, and told how they had had more trouble to meet the quotas than many other villages. They had mainly earned their living by fishing before the foreigners had come, and the soldiers had confiscated almost all of their canoes. Making new ones takes skill, he explained, skill that the village now lacks.

Right then one of the women behind him took a step forward and began to speak. The flurry that came out was quenched, just as soon as it had begun, by the chief who pinched her on the forearm. The woman squealed, crossed her arms over her chest and fell back.

"What did the woman say?"

"I didn't quite catch her words," Lucas said.

The chief guessed the topic of their conversation correctly, and dismissed the whole mishappening. All three women were from another village, and had been a rare gift from the white devil. Whether as an effort to build a more amicable relationship, or simply to entice the chief to work with him and give him what he was owned, that was something the chief didn't know. And yet the chief was bitter about it, as he had only received three women, whereas the Chief of the neighbouring village had received four, and prettier ones at that too. He hadn't been rewarded equally.

Polygamy was something that the Europeans were keen to see swiped under the rug, eventually at least, but it wasn't Roger's place to judge. He instead asked where the women were from.

The chief said he didn't know or care. His two sons had died fighting the foreigners, and he had lost his daughter to the sleeping sickness. He only hoped that one of his new wives would still bear him a son when things would improve, and added with a dry laugh that his wish might take time, more than he had.

For a while, Roger scribbled down his notes on paper and thought on what had been said.

Children were a rarity among the locals, especially those children who in Europe were at the age to attend schools, if their parents' socio-economic standing so permitted. There were none such children in this village. What few Roger could spot in the crowd couldn't have been older than three or four, or then they were only a year or two away from becoming adults. He couldn't see a single baby in the crowd, and the lone cry he had heard earlier very likely marked the baby as the only one in the entire village, and the third he had so far taken notice of in the area.

All of that matched the timeframe when the worst of the rubber terror had taken place. It had claimed an entire generation of unborn children from hopeful parents.

At the thought of it, Roger realized something else. Something more disturbing. It was a thought that had so far eluded him, but now it came clear to him. The accounts he had collected in the last week and a half matched what he had heard on his way to the lake just a month ago. The locals who had fled a considerable distance to escape the impossible India-rubber quotas placed on them. They had only left out one part: had it been five years since they left, or less?

The locals here were also subjected to quotas. The only difference were the products the quotas were placed on. And if those quotas were maintained so rigorously around Lake Mantumba, with captivity, corporeal punishment and bribes, the same would likely hold true for other parts of the Free State as well. Or with worse means still.

Roger barely had time to open his mouth and give voice to his thoughts when he caught a motioning hand in the corner of his eye. Shouts broke around him, and the locals who had just dared to venture out to meet the two missionaries rushed back into the jungle's safety. John sprang and growled in a low voice, something that could only be seen but not heard over the clamour.

The chief let out a deep sigh and shook his head in disapproval. Men armed with spears and tower shields made out of bark rushed to him. They didn't point their weapons' sharp ends at the two white foreigners, but made it clear that they should maintain their distance. One of the women swung her arm across the air and yelled something before they left. Roger didn't need a translation to understand that the word was an insult aimed at them.

"What is...what's the meaning of this?" Lucas stammered between short, quick steps. "Someone else must be coming to the village."

"Someone else? Who?"

"I have no clue. Gaspard maybe? Or soldiers. Someone they don't trust like they did us," Roger suggested. "Come. Let's go see by the shore. Whoever it is, I hope they have a good reason for scaring off the locals like that."

A large canoe approached the village. It was still far, but Roger could make out a man standing at the forefront. He didn't need to pick up the pair of binoculars from the beached steamer to differentiate the man's blue uniform.

"Who are they? Can you see them this far?" Lucas asked while attempting to fix his eyeglasses.

"They are soldiers."

"The Force Publique?"

"Yes."

"The few soldiers that remain in Bikoro rarely leave the place anymore. What are they doing here all of a sudden?"

Roger left the question unanswered.

The canoe approached the shore slowly. It was rowed by several soldiers and few others who lacked the uniforms, likely workers who had been assembled at the job on a moment's notice. Only the man at the front didn't participate in their collective effort. He seemed to lack the patience to wait for the cumbersome canoe to beach, and jumped to the water. From there, he waded ashore. The dramatic act didn't save him much time, and only made his uniform take on a darker shade from below his hipline.

"Mr Casement, good, you're here. And Mr Peerenboom also," David said, and then directed his words at the latter, "we were looking for you."

"You were looking for me?" Lucas repeated.

"Yes. We need you back to Bikoro now."

"What has happened?"

"Something important. Please, you need to come now," David almost demanded and jerked his head towards the lake. "We can go over the details on our way back there, but we're leaving right now."

* * *

"We must bury him here," Gaspard announced.

"Absolutely not," Cécile protested. "We should send his body back to Europe for proper burials."

"His body would only rot on the way back."

"It's still better than leaving it rot here."

"No European should have to call Africa's restless soil their resting place," Lucas commented.

"It could take weeks to even get Henrik's body to the coast, and then two more months to get him to Sweden," Roger said. "There wouldn't be anything left of him to bury by then."

"Yes, the consul is right," Gaspard agreed. "It's far from ideal, but better to call Africa one's tomb than none at all."

Henrik had died. When and to what, that wasn't clear, but it was also unimportant. All that was certain was that he had gone unceremoniously. The body had yet to be moved from the guestroom's bed, from the flimsy bed sheets that it had become stuck to, but it had already been nibbled at. Even now several dozen flies buzzed around it despite Cécile's irregular attempts at shooing them away, and many more clambered over the pale, pockmarked skin marbled with decaying veins. The face was swollen and ready to burst like a grape. White oval-shaped eggs lined the fishlike lips, dry nostrils and half-empty eye sockets. Henrik must've been dead for at least a day now: it didn't take longer for maggots to appear on an unattended feast.

The heat and mosquitoes must've been too much for him. Some made it, others didn't. Usually it were the young and eager, the ones who came to Congo in search of a grand adventure exploring the unknown and fighting off natives, who ended up dead from an insect bite within a month or two. Unlike in the best-selling storybooks of Europe, there was no wild nature to tame here or treasures that would make one an overnight millionaire. Everything that Congo offered would have to be paid for in blood and sweat.

"To think that there was a dead person in the room next to mine for God knows how many days, and I didn't notice," Roger said aloud after a moment of silence. "At worst, I noticed a slight smell, but I thought nothing of it."

"Don't beat yourself up over it, you couldn't have known with how busy you've been," Gaspard said and breathed in. "All in favour of burying Henrik as soon as possible?"

"No, no, and no," Cécile said. "No one is going to get buried here."

"Cécile, look at me," Gaspard said and turned to face her. When she didn't lift her eyes from the body, he took hold of her hanging chin, forced her to look at his eyes and said, "Wife, I know it's hard to look at what's left of him, but the only way Henrik will know a measure of peace is if we bury him here and now."

"As much as I'd want to see this poor boy returned to his parents, Gaspard and Roger make a good point," Lucas weighed in after a moment of hesitation. "I am willing to perform the necessary burial rites."

"But…but wasn't he Protestant? How can you perform those rites? He needs a Protestant priest," Cécile said and absent-mindedly shooed Gaspard's hand away.

"When it's about emergency rites like this, distinctions like that don't make much of a difference."

"Cécile, the only thing that matters is to grant the boy a measure of peace," Roger said and watched a particularly large fly crawl out of Henrik's left ear.

Cécile didn't answer. Gaspard turned to Lucas and proceeded to say, "Good. We're in an agreement then. Death's an unfortunate and dirty business, but one that happens from time to time. I hope that if I'd meet the same fate in Congo that I'd be buried here."

"I'll go get all the necessary scriptures and the rosary from the chapel," Lucas said. "I think that, under the circumstances, we can skip the vigil for the deceased and the viewing of the body."

"In the meanwhile, Alphonse can carry the body to the forest and prepare a grave."

"No, you can't possibly do that," Cécile woke from her stupor to protest.

"Why?"

The four were alone by the guesthouse, but she pulled in closer to Gaspard, as if afraid that someone would overhear them. She lowered her voice, "The natives are cannibals, don't you remember? I saw how he eyed the body this morning."

Gaspard had to stifle his laugh. It only got Cécile to raise her voice, "What? I'm serious. If we hadn't been here to keep an eye on him, Alphonse would've already led all the other savages here. If you let him bury Henrik, then all of that was for nothing. He'd only reveal the location to others, and they'd have him dug up the moment we'd turn our backs on it, and…"

"And what? Eat it? Just like Julienne ate Henrik's meal?" Gaspard dismissed. "Look at the body. No one would touch that."

"Please. At least, have someone else do it, like…like David, for example."

"Why him?"

"Henrik was an officer, wasn't he?" Roger brought up. "It'd make sense to have his soldiers bury him."

"Yes! And the soldiers have at least some idea of discipline that should make them refrain from eating what's left of the poor."

Her sentence was cut short when she turned around to look at the body. She leaned forward and let out an involuntary gag, like she was about to vomit. Her face flushed red before she gasped, "Oh God, just the idea makes me sick."

Gaspard took hold of her hand and gave in, "Very well. I'll have David do that with some others, if it makes you feel better."

* * *

The funeral took place around sunset. Besides the only four remaining Europeans in Bikoro, the funeral was attended only by David and some other soldiers. They had managed to dig a shallow grave in an unremarkable place some distance from the mansion, near the jungle's edge. The setting sun made the shadows stretch over the wet ground and reach into emptiness.

There hadn't been much reading or hymns, only a few that Lucas and Cécile had chosen without much thought put into them. When Lucas read the last of the prayers, the soldiers picked up their shovels and lopped wet dirt over the body. Several flies crawled out from under the white cloth covering the body to avoid being buried with the minor noble. Their hatchlings wouldn't be as lucky.

The small crowd dispersed soon afterwards. Gaspard and Cécile headed straight back to the mansion. She had tried her best to keep the tears at bay, but Roger could hear her sobbing on the way back.

"Roger, a moment of your time, if I may," Lucas asked and approached him. "I have a feeling that there was something more you wanted to ask the chieftain in the village today."

"Yes, there was."

"What was it?"

Roger told him of what had occurred to him earlier. He mentioned his fears that quotas similar to the ones imposed by Gaspard around the lake were commonplace all over the Free State, as were the punishments associated with them. Then he lowered his voice a notch to ask about the only missing piece from the puzzle: if the mutilation of hands, something that he still lacked any proof of, was still going on somewhere deeper in Congo.

Lucas listened to him attentively, and then spoke with a lazy voice, "If you ever had a chance to pry that truth from Gaspard, I'd say it's gone by now."

"How come?"

"Today's interruption doesn't matter in the least," Lucas explained. "You talked to me about your intentions to leave Mantumba, and you also dismissed my suggestion to talk with Gaspard about the use of the whip as futile."

"I did, yes."

"I think you're right in saying that you're only wasting your time here, and that you won't get anything else out of Gaspard. He's been disinclined to work with you from the beginning, and he won't change his mind,"

"Are you imploring me to leave?"

"I am," Lucas said and struck his cane in the soft dirt. "You know I don't approve of the things Gaspard has done around here, but there's nothing I've been able to do about them. You, on the other hand, can. And the sooner you get your work done and return to Europe, the sooner they'll learn of what's happening here."

"Yes, those are my thoughts," Roger said, "and when heard from your mouth like that, they make more sense. I'll have one final chat with the chief of the post tomorrow, and then leave."

"Whatever happens, it has been good to get to know you. I hope we'll see each other one day again," Lucas said and extended his hand a bit to the side.

Roger took hold of it and shook gently.

10. Faithful

"Okay, so this was way back in the day when the foreigners were just arriving to Nzere. My village met with this…"

"How old are you, old man? Four hundred years?" a voice interrupted. A commotion of laughter followed.

"Not quite," the first voice joined in the laugh, "closer to a hundred."

"You don't look even half the age!"

"That's what ten years working for the whites does to you."

Another burst of laughter echoed under the setting sun. Nsala was there to share a bowl of boiled cassava and a vessel of dark brown water with the others. Ashes still simmered in a small fire pit that they had used to prepare the same meal they had eaten daily for as long as any could remember.

"Alright, alright, enough jokes," the old man continued behind a grin. "This first foreigner that I saw with my own eyes twenty years ago, he didn't come from the south, no. He came from the north."

"You're still joking, old man," Nsala brought up.

"Yeah. How did he come from upstream if all the others have come from downstream?"

"Most of you are too young to even remember it, but that's where the Zanzibar slavers came from. They had helped this white and his men through the jungle to Nzere."

"They worked together. It's like I've told you so many times, the whites are no better than the Zanzibaris," someone called out. "The only difference is the colour of their skin."

"Nobody has ever disagreed with you on that," another said.

"A slaver is a slaver," the old man agreed and continued. "This white came to our village by Nzere. He spoke a lot and fast, and I feel that much of what he wanted to say was lost in between the lines. Anyway, this Mr Stanley, I think that was his name, asked the chieftain to put his mark on a piece of paper, and gave him a bottle of something strong in exchange for that. Now, we didn't think much of it, so the chieftain agreed, thinking that he'd get the better of that strange man, but ten years later, other white foreigners came, tapped their fingers on that exact same paper and said we were obliged to work for them for the rest of our days because this Stanley had given the chieftain that bottle."

The old man paused to build up tension. Instead of a dramatic ending that the small crowd was waiting for, he swung his arm in the air, looked down and said, "I'm telling you, whatever was in that bottle must've been worth a lot."

Laughter erupted once again.

"Did you at least get a sip of this drink fit for Gods?" someone managed to ask.

"Of course not. It was for the chieftain and his family alone. His kids didn't like it, though."

"Come to think of it, Nsala, have you ever had a chance to taste anything the whites keep for themselves now that you work at the mansion?" another asked.

"Yeah, and what's up with those weird clothes that I've seen you use? They look unbearably uncomfortable."

Every day after finishing his work, Nsala clambered out of the shirt and pants and switched to the simple loincloth that he was more familiar with. He still didn't like the European clothes, and sitting around with the others as the only person dressed in them would've made him stand out too much from the crowd for his own liking.

He dismissed the others' questions, "The devil gave the clothes to me when he took me into his mansion. He thought going without them was 'too uncivilized' for him. And for the drink, ah, they call it wine, and no, I haven't had a chance to try it."

"Yet."

"I hope you don't end up selling one of us to Gaspard for a taste of it."

"Not to worry, our own chieftains already did that!" Nsala announced.

The laughter continued. Nsala shook his head with a wide grin. He then reached with his hand for a scoop of cassava and stuck it inside his mouth. The laughter continued for a short while before it died down all of a sudden. Smiles faded and mouths stopped in place, half-chewed food still inside. Heads turned to face the same direction, eyes nailed onto something.

It took Nsala a few seconds to follow the others' example. He turned around and saw a lone soldier walking on the road. He carried a shovel over his shoulder.

"What's a soldier doing here at this time?" a whisper asked. "Maybe he's on a patrol?" another answered.

"No, they never come through here at this time."

"What's the shovel for? Did they bury someone?"

"Did one of us die?"

"Don't be stupid, they'd just toss the body somewhere in the jungle, not bury it."

"Are you saying someone else died?"

"A foreigner?"

"It must be. What else would the shovel be for?"

Nsala didn't have to join in with the others' guessing. He knew exactly who had been buried. He had been there this morning to see the body.

"Look. He…he has a whip on his belt."

"A chicote."

"I haven't seen one in months."

The small crowd turned silent when they realized the soldier made his way towards them.

Up closer Nsala recognized the soldier as the same brute he had come to know. This time, however, he had hints of reserved anger on his face instead of the usual calm indifference.

David stopped some metres from them. He breathed in and out before letting the shovel fall down at his feet.

"Go, leave, before I change my mind," he ordered and then looked into Nsala. "Not you, you'll stay."

Eyes darted around, unsure of what to do at the unexpected request. "Now!"

The others didn't need further convincing. They squirmed their way into the shadows. "What's this about?" Nsala asked and stood up as David walked closer.

"Quiet. You'll only speak when I ask you to speak. You're not in the British consul's presence."

"Mr Casement? What has he...?"

"Gaspard ordered me to bury Henrik," David interrupted, "and when he did, he told me you should've done it, but his wife put me on the job instead. Do you understand what I'm saying?"

Nsala nodded carefully before David added, "You know why? Because she thinks you're a cannibal."

"Is that why you're angry? Because you buried Henrik? What does that have to do with...?"

He didn't expect the sudden jab just below his ribcage. At one moment, he was confused and the next on his knees, eyes wide open. He gasped for air, but only managed to let out a rasp. A ball of spit ran down his chin.

"I thought you understood French! What part of 'you'll only speak when I ask you to speak' did you not understand?"

Nsala gripped his side and stood up. He looked around, at the huddled onlookers and figures squatting inside their huts, but no one was there with him.

"Yes, I had to bury Henrik." David continued in a softer tone. "Maybe he wasn't a friend, but the closest one I had. And I had to bury him. I had to do that because you wouldn't do it."

"You just said Gaspard wouldn't let me."

"Do you know how it feels to bury a friend?"

"No, but I remember how you cut off my daughter's hand. I remember how in the next morning I sat on a porch, one foot on wet grass, tired from a sleepless night, and stared at a stump of what remained of a small hand," Nsala said back.

"It's already been several months since that happened. How do you expect me to forget something like that?"

"It's not the same."

"How is it not the same?"

"Your daughter is still alive, is she not?"

"I haven't seen her in months. I don't know."

"Well, Henrik is dead. I know that for certain because I buried him."

"Henrik was never your friend," Nsala dismissed. "None of the whites are."

"Not to you, no, but he was to me."

"You know why? Because you gave away everything you had to the whites! Your home, your language, even your name. Officer Fidèle, huh?"

"You don't know the first thing about me," David said. His wandering eyes focused on the lone man in front of him and his body tensed up.

"You're just a tool for the Belgians. And you were that to Henrik as well."

"No. No, you're wrong!" David yelled again. "The Europeans have given me more than you could ever understand. My parents, my whole village, they abandoned me, while the Belgians took me in. They took care of me. Do you understand? That's what they told me."

"Your own parents feared the Belgians and ran away. They would fear you as…"

A sudden jab cut him off. Nsala fell down again.

"You're not the same as me! You're not the same as me!" David panted. "You can go back to swinging from trees and stuffing bananas into your mouth all day, but I know the world's bigger than that! The Europeans have shown me that. And now one of them is dead. My friend is dead!"

Nsala looked up and opened his mouth, but a foot pushed him down before he could say anything more. It held him there as more and more fearful eyes appeared from the approaching darkness to see the commotion.

"You're not brave, just like you weren't brave when begging for your daughter's hand to be spared. If anything, you only have yourself to blame for what happened to her. But even after that, she still has her life," David continued while his voice cracked down to a sob. "Henrik was innocent. And I had to bury him. I had to bury my friend, because you wouldn't do it. No one should have to bury their friend."

Nsala bit his teeth together and managed to ask, "Then what do you think I felt when I buried my daughter's…"

Right then he felt something sharp slash against his buttocks. Coarse leather bit down to his muscle and made him scream.

"When we're done, you're to salute me formally, or you'll end up back on the ground," David snorted in between the lashes. "They say you Ntombas are cannibals. Cécile seemed sure of it, but I'm not. However it may be, you don't want to end up as the others' next meal. You at least still have some muscles to your bones. So pull yourself through!"

After the initial screaming and struggling, Nsala's head collapsed down. He fell quiet. His eyelids felt heavy. Faintly gleaming eyes watched on in the dark, just as silent and helpless as the lone victim on the ground, before they faded out.

11. Pet Monkey

Raindrops fell down from the clouded sky and rang against the living room's large windows. The golden, soft light that had flooded the room two weeks ago when Roger and Gaspard had met here for the first time was gone, and in its place was only monotonous grey and uneasy silence. All of it enhanced the impact that King Leopold's silver lined portrait had over the room, and made his eyes hang heavy over the space. Only the bulldog John seemed unaware of the heavy atmosphere, sleeping soundly at Roger's feet.

"I'm planning to move on," Roger was the first to say.

"Moving on? When exactly?" Gaspard asked.

"Today, in a couple of hours. My steamer is small and fast. It should be able to reach the Congo River by nightfall. It will also help clear the pier for the passenger ship that arrives here by afternoon. It's the one that…"

"That Cécile will take to Boma, yes."

"I intend to be gone by then, to avoid creating a one of a kind traffic jam at your pier."

"And you only now decided to bring up the matter with me?"

"Apologies for the suddenness, but I came to that conclusion after talking to Lucas last night, after the funeral,"

Roger explained. "I feel that I've seen everything that Bikoro and the surrounding areas have to offer for my work."

"Are you headed back to Boma?"

"Not yet. First I plan to journey deeper inland."

"Deeper inland?" Gaspard repeated. "Were you not satisfied with your findings in Bikoro?"

"I feel that my report could still use some work before I present it to the parliament back home."

"Do you have any particular place in mind then? Most of the land north of here is owned by the Free State, just like in Bikoro. I doubt you'd find things any different there."

"Before I left Boma, I compiled a list of all the places I intended to visit. There's not much left on it, actually, only a few areas given to private companies."

"I see. There are indeed a couple of areas like that north of here. Which company's area do you intend to visit?"

"The Abir Congo Company. Since Bikoro doesn't produce any wild India-rubber anymore…"

"I don't."

"I feel that it'd be important to visit some part of Congo that still does. And after that, I'll return to Boma to finalize the report."

"I understand," Gaspard said. "If I recall correctly, the British shareholders left the company some five years ago, but I imagine you must have some vested interest in seeing how the company is doing given its shared history with your countrymen."

"Not my countrymen, but 'subjects of the same crown'," Roger corrected. "I think those were the exact words you used when we met for the first time."

Gaspard gave his words a slow nod and looked outside. He spoke to the rain outside, "In any case, I hope you have enjoyed your time in Bikoro, and that it has helped you in preparing your report."

"It has helped me, although I cannot say that I've enjoyed my stay here as much as I hoped I would've."

"Have I been an ungenerous host or treated you badly?"

"No, not at all. I meant the conditions that I've witnessed the locals suffering from. The high amount of work, the unnecessarily cruel bodily punishments, such as imprisonment and lashings, and the inadequate compensation for the labour they provide, among other things."

Before he continued, Roger paid attention on how Gaspard didn't react or comment his mention of lashings in any way.

"Well, we've already gone through these matters several times. No need to dwell on them now. I've assembled all of my findings in a letter that I intend to hand over to the governor-general when I return to Boma," Roger said and reached inside his pocket. He unfolded a piece of paper, presented it to Gaspard and said, "You can read the letter now, if you wish, so you will be aware of all the things that you could strive to improve."

Gaspard looked at him, raised an open palm in the air and declined, "You can leave the letter on the table. I'll go through it later and post it to Boma with today's passenger ship. If you're headed deeper into the country, this way the latter will arrive to Boma earlier."

"I mean no disrespect," Roger said and pulled the letter back, "but I'd rather see the letter delivered to the governor-general personally."

"Of course."

"However, despite my aforementioned disappointments, I'm relieved to say that based on what I've seen of your trading post and the surrounding areas, the Mantumba district doesn't live up to the reports of mutilations and violence that I've heard."

"It's like I've already told you: those reports are nothing but bland propaganda meant to defame King Leopold."

"I deeply hope that you're right, I do, but I will reserve my final judgment until the end. And I also offer my condolences for Henrik's unexpected death."

"Thank you, consul. Truth be told, he wasn't very good at his job as the subordinate official, but it's always sad to see a young life wasted away like that. He didn't like Congo one bit."

"No, he didn't. You could see that clearly from the first time we met."

The sound of raindrops banging against glass and roof tiles filled the room as both gathered their thoughts. In between them there was a faint sound of creaking stairs.

Eventually Gaspard broke the silence, "Tell me, consul, before you go, have you enjoyed your time in Congo?"

"I think I already said that I haven't."

"No, I didn't mean your stay in Bikoro. I meant your career in Congo."

"Oh," Roger began, "well, not really. I'm almost forty years old, and still stuck working in Africa. I've...an impression that you feel the same."

"I do."

"Then at least it's one thing that we have in common."

"It seems so," Gaspard said in a low voice before raising his eyes to meet Roger's. "Should we drink to that? To your report? That it will change the other one's career. Either it will help you secure a better post, or bring me recognition for helping clear the king's name."

"That will all depend on how the public reacts to my dry report back home."

"Then it's settled," Gaspard said with a forced smile. "We have our differences, but it's all behind us now."

He turned his head towards the hallway and hollered Julienne by name. There was no response. He called her by name again, but was met with the same silence.

He mumbled something to himself and stood up. Roger and John followed. Gaspard called for Julienne one more time in the hallway, until Nsala came to meet him. Roger paid attention on how he stood with a curved back and appeared tired.

"What do you need, sir?"

"I didn't call for you. Where's Julienne?"

"In the kitchen with Cécile, sir."

"In the kitchen? Why?"

"Julienne was supposed to bring tea and biscuits to her room, but hadn't had the time yet because we were cleaning the floors together," Nsala explained. He stood in a slight slouch, and the speech came to him with some effort. "She took Julienne by the wrist and dragged her to the kitchen."

"Not with this again," Gaspard moaned to himself.

"Did it have anything to do with you?" Roger asked.

"No. I just kept cleaning because it didn't seem to concern me," Nsala said and paused. "Does it concern me as well?"

The unusual lethargy that had troubled Gaspard the entire morning disappeared. He almost pushed Nsala to the side and made his way towards the dining room just in time to hear a shout.

Gaspard rushed past the table and slammed the kitchen door open.

Julienne took support from a table and covered her left cheek with her hand. It was the same cheek where Roger had spotted a bruise before. Cécile loomed over her, the flat tea pan and assorted biscuits.

"Cécile, what are you doing?" Gaspard blurted out.

"I was having a chat with Julienne."

"Weren't you supposed to be packing your luggage upstairs?"

"I was, but I got thirsty and hungry. This...monkey was supposed to bring me tea and biscuits, but of course she wouldn't, so I had to come down here to ask after them."

"You've hit Julienne. You shouldn't abuse the servants."

She huffed with disbelief, "I can't believe you're saying something like that after everything you've done to your workers."

"You don't reward a good worker with a cane."

"How about a secret lover?"

"Where did you get a ridiculous idea like that from?"

"From your secret lover, of course," Cécile said. "The moment I hit her she mumbled something about you, and then wouldn't explain what it was!"

Gaspard looked at Julienne. She had understood enough of their exchange, and returned him a pleading look, asking for help.

"Look at her. She's scared of you. She just was trying to call me here to stop you from hitting her without a reason."

"Because she knew you'd take her side, again!"

"Yes, because you're accusing her, again, without anything to back your imaginations."

Cécile grasped Julienne by the wrist, pulled her up and slammed her hand over the table with strength beyond what her bloated appearance would've suggested. She held the hand there and reached for a kitchen knife. Gaspard took a hurried step forward.

"Calm down, wife. You're going too far."

John let out a sharp bark, and before the growling dog could do anything else, Roger took it into his arms.

Cécile held the knife in the air and panted. In between the breaths, she managed to say, "There's nothing wrong with cutting off a Negro's hand. You've done the same before, haven't you? Many times over! What's one more hand going to mean to you?"

"Wife, you're only seeing what you want to see."

"Am I?"

"If there's one thing that I am, it's loyal. Devout," Gaspard said and drove his right thumb against his chest. "I've lost count of all the times I've asked you to stay here with me together, as a husband and a wife, instead of running off to Boma every second month for your own amusement."

"All that time has just given you time to warm our bed with this monkey."

"All that time has only made us grow apart. Don't you see it, wife? I want…"

"Don't you dare call me your wife!"

"You here with me, by my side where you should be."

"We have nothing in common."

He took a step towards her, this one slower and more deliberate. "Please, stop crying."

"I'm not crying!"

"You are, wife. Now stop doing that, please."

"Like you care what others think. Like you ever cared about me!" she yelled and turned the kitchen knife at him.

He took another step forward. He was close enough that she could've stabbed him, but instead her hand began to shake. Her lips trembled. Her grip on Julienne's hand loosened, and Julienne rushed out of the room. Gaspard reached out, but stayed his hand and looked back at Cécile.

She let go of the knife and fell down sobbing. The knife fell on the table. Gaspard kneeled down on the stone floor besides her.

"Love, you know I've always cared about you, and will always do so."

Gaspard took hold of her hand. Incoherent words began to form on her lips in between the heavy breaths and tears. It took Cécile a moment to raise her head, shook and stutter, "No, you don't. You claim to be a good Christian? You have an affair with that…that…monkey, and you claim to be a good Christian?"

"You know that's…"

"Don't preach to me about marital loyalty."

"You know that's not true."

"It is. I know it is! Papa was right when he said I should've married someone else. Anyone else. The only thing you care about is your precious Leopold!" she shouted and stood up clumsily. On the way up, she tried to push Gaspard over, but only managed to nudge him back a bit.

"Where are you going?"

"Back home to Belgium, with my family," she said before rushing out of the room, past Roger and Nsala. She didn't glance at either one.

Gaspard was left alone on the kitchen floor. Only now did he seem to realize the presence of the two onlookers. He stood up and brushed his white shirt with his hands, more out of habit than anything else.

"I apologize you had to see that happen on your last day," he said to Roger. "There's no need to apologize for something like that."

"I feel that I must," Gaspard said, lifted and shook the tea pan to gauge its contents. "Alphonse, prepare two – no, three – cups of tea, and bring them to the living room."

"Mr Bunschoten, there's no need for this."

"There is. We shouldn't part on a sour note like this, and without having the toast that you suggested. Perhaps not with the same wine that we enjoyed on the first time, but at least with something nonetheless."

"If you insist, then," Roger said, "but who's the third cup for?"

"Julienne. The way my wife has been treating her lately, it makes me ashamed. She's only doing her job after all, and facing unwarranted abuse from it."

Roger gave his words a silent, careful nod. They left the room together while Nsala stayed behind to prepare tea like nothing out of ordinary had taken place.

They found Julienne hiding behind one of the living room's chairs. She didn't need much convincing to come out and to sit around the wicker table with Roger and Gaspard. Soon Nsala brought them the tea. He didn't get to share in the drink, and assumed a by now familiar stance near a wall in case there would be need for him. Roger noted how standing in place seemed to be more difficult to him than before.

Julienne drank too much of the hot beverage at once. She pulled the cup away from her lips and splashed some of its contents on the floor. It must've been her first time trying the beverage. Gaspard instructed her to sip it slowly, more carefully. Once she got the hang of it, she hardly lowered the cup from her hands. A red hue appeared on her cheeks.

Roger watched her at the corner of his eye. After a moment, he turned to Gaspard and asked him, "What did Cécile mean when she threatened to cut off Julienne's hand? She said that there was nothing wrong with it because you've done the same."

"I don't know. I think she meant the bodily punishments, as you have called them."

"But that's not the same as cutting off a hand."

"Of course it's not. She exaggerated. She must've thought that wanton mutilation like that would be the same as imprisonment, but it's not," Gaspard said and shook his head in disapproval. "I'm sure you've noticed in your short time here how Cécile has a bad habit of working herself up into a hysteria at times, just like she did during our dinner party."

"I remember."

"This recent…incident, was no different. She'll calm down, I'm sure of it. She just needs some time alone."

"Let's hope so."

Gaspard sipped some of the tea and switched topic: "When were you planning to leave exactly?"

"In an hour or so. I'm hoping the rain would die down a bit."

Gaspard gave his words a hum that was devoid of anything meaningful. Roger noticed how Nsala had shook in place at the mention of those words, like a spider had been crawling down his back.

Not soon after the sound of stumping feet rang down the hallway's stairs. Cécile passed by the broad doorway with two luggage in tow. Both fresh and dried out tears glistened on her face. She didn't even stop to glance at them.

Gaspard shot up and ran after her.

"Wife, where are you going?" Roger heard him ask in the hallway. "To wait for the ship," her voice answered.

"In the rain?"

"Yes."

"You'll only get a flu."

"I don't care."

"Please, wife, think this through now. Come sit with us in…"

"Your pet monkey can share the table with you now."

That was the last Roger heard of her. A door creaked open and the sound of rain got a bit louder for a few seconds before getting muffled again. All that was left then was the sound of an echoing thunder in the distance. Roger's eyes moved to Nsala and then to Julienne. Both seemed just as indifferent at what had happened.

The defeated Gaspard dragged himself back into his chair. He sloughed in it and leaned his head against his right arm. He left the rest of his tea untouched and cold.

"The weather's getting worse," Roger noted after a while. "It is," Gaspard said to the floor.

"There's no point in setting sail now. If it's fine by you, I'd prefer to stay until the evening and see where the storm goes."

"I think you'll have to wait until the morning."

"I fear as much."

"Never mind. I'll have the servants prepare some dinner for three."

"Do you think Cécile will come around?"

"I do. Ever since we came here five years ago, she's complained about how much she hates it here in Congo, but I can't see why she'd want to spend the day sitting alone in a torrent," Gaspard spoke and rubbed his forehead. "I'm sorry you had to see all that."

The outdoor opened again. Three pairs of wet boots creaked on the planks before three men, one white and two black, appeared by the doorway. Roger recognized them as his steamer's crew. The European explained in English that they had come inside away from the rain, and because some woman had started to scream at them to leave her alone.

* * *

The rain kept coming the whole day. By evening, the thunder had gone away and the rain had slowed down to a drizzle, but the raindrops kept racing down the windows' uneven surfaces and damp air oozed through the thin wooden walls. Cécile's steamer had finally arrived by the dock and set down the anchor to wait for what little light the morning would bring with it. Usually it would've been Gaspard's job to welcome the odd passengers and see to it that the steamer had enough firewood to continue on its journey, but David received that honour for the first time. This time there hadn't been any passengers who would've gotten off at Bikoro, no itinerant missionaries, rotating officials, or soldiers posted to another place, and none of the others had wanted to even go ashore to stretch their legs in the rain. Only soaked Cécile got aboard, opting for the first time in her life to sleep on a foldable mattress inside a flimsy cabin with strangers instead of a proper bed in the mansion.

Roger had kept his words and stayed for the night, either because he respected Cécile's wish for privacy, or because he wanted to see how things would turn out in the following days. Nsala wasn't sure which one, but his mind kept returning to that thought while cleaning dishes in the kitchen alone. Either way, it seemed like he was really leaving. He wasn't sure how to feel about it.

Together with Julienne, he had prepared a simple meal of cassava and fish to Gaspard and Roger. The two had passed the evening in awkward silence broken only by Gaspard's occasional apology for today's events and Roger's recurring reassurance that none was needed. Roger had then headed back to his guestroom, and after that, Gaspard had instructed Nsala to clean everything before he had headed off and asked Julienne to follow. Her body had relaxed and her gaze sunk down, like the request was something she had been expecting.

It didn't take Nsala long to finish his work for the day. He washed his hands and blew off the oil lamp before heading out to the small hut some distance away that he had come to call as his new home.

It had taken him some time to get used to moving around the mansion's dark rooms and hallway after sunset. The building wasn't particularly large, but the many carpets, tables and pieces of furniture that melted into the dark space had at first presented obstacles that were new to him. This particular evening however there was something new he hadn't seen before: a faint yellow light was coming from one of the rooms, the living room. He decided to peek in.

He saw Gaspard slouching on a chair, the same one where he had sat during the day. On the table was a small oil lamp. Julienne was there too, standing between the two. Her white, worn dress, the same one she always wore, was folded halfway down and left her upper body bare.

She stood there, her right flank bathed in light, still as a statue and just as indifferent, while he massaged her breasts with his fist.

"Have you kept taking that medicine that should stop pregnancies?" Gaspard asked.

Julienne gave him a shy nod.

"Good. You're going to need more of that going forward," Gaspard said and forced a sour smile across his lips.

12. The Unwanted

Nsala found Roger leaning backwards on a wooden rocking chair just outside the guest room that was reserved for him. The narrow terrace had just enough space to afford him that, and the overhanging roof kept the drizzle away from a small oil lamp that illuminated half of his face and a pile of papers he was going through. At times, his pen's metal clip glittered in the light.

He was oblivious towards the hunched figure that approached him. The bulldog John, on the other hand, was roused from his slumber by the sound of splashing sandal soles in the mud, and caught his master's attention as well.

"Nsala," Roger said and lowered the papers, "what brings you here?"

"Mr Casement, sir," Nsala hesitated and stammered. "There's...there's something that I would like to show to you, sir."

"Show me?"

"Yes."

"Could it perhaps wait until morning, when there's light and hopefully no more rain?"

"No, sir, it…it can't," Nsala stuttered as raindrops ran down his nose and back. They made him do an involuntary shiver.

"Why not?" Roger asked and took a smoking pipe from a table next to the oil lamp and papers. "And by all means, come out of the rain. There's enough space under the roof for us both."

"Thank you, sir," Nsala said and stepped forward. His sandals left mud stains on the polished planks. The flame's yellow light picked on the edges of his shrivelled face.

"Nsala, what's gotten into you? You're addressing me formally again."

"I'm sorry. It's just that there's a lot on my mind at the moment."

"Does it have to do with what you wanted to show me?"

"It does, sir. But we'd have to go there now, because otherwise I couldn't show it to you."

"Why not?"

"Because you're gone by tomorrow, aren't you?"

"I won't leave until noon," Roger assured with a puff from his pipe. "So whatever it is, I'm sure we'll have time for it in the morning."

"No, we wouldn't, because I fear there wouldn't be another chance to show this place to you before you leave," Nsala hurried to say.

"A place?" Roger repeated. "This something that you want to show to me is a place?"

Nsala gave a slight nod as his answer. Roger looked past the rain at the lone light shining from the mansion's living room's windows. He smacked his lips a couple of times before asking what Gaspard was doing at this time of the evening.

"He's reading news, sir, and drinking tea."

"Thinking on it, if you want me to follow you into the rain, I could use some tea first."

"No, sir. Gaspard…he asked to be left alone. That's why I was heading home early."

"I see," Roger said, "but then what made you to decide to show this place to me now, and not, for example, earlier?"

"Because going through all of those news is going to keep him distracted for a while, and everyone else around is sleeping or staying inside."

"Some secret place, then, that Gaspard hasn't wanted me to see?"

"Yes, but it's…it's easier to just show it to you."

"Now you got me intrigued. I'd still rather wait for morning, but if you absolutely insist on going there now, we can go. I however expect you to explain on the way there what this secret place is," Roger said and stood up. "Just give me a moment first."

He shook the ashes from his pipe, took it and the papers back inside the guest room, and returned with a small umbrella in hand. He apologized that there was only enough space for one person under it. It didn't matter to Nsala, or to John, who leaped after his master's footsteps in the wet mud.

Roger held the lamp's burning flame in front of him. At times, an odd raindrop feel into the feeble flame and sizzled. The light was barely enough for them to tell the muddy road apart from the surrounding muck and grass, but Roger could tell from the direction they had taken that they were headed for Bomenga.

"This place where we're going to has to do with the history of Bikoro, Bomenga and the entire Lake Mantumba. It's the side of the story that Gaspard hasn't shown to you yet, and would never show to you," Nsala said to the rain after a while. "You'll just have to trust me that it's important."

"I do trust you, Nsala. You've been of great help to me. What you've already told me, how most of Bikoro was razed down to make room for the Belgians' ambitions, and how most of the original inhabitants died during the rubber terror, all of it has been immensely important to my work."

"There was actually more I wanted to tell you, back on the day you called me brave."

"Only you didn't."

"No, I didn't."

"Why not? What happened?"

"David," Nsala spelled out. "He came to see you."

"I doubted as much," Roger recalled. "When I asked you afterwards if there was something more you wanted to say, you said that you had forgotten what it was because it wasn't important."

"Seeing David reminded me that I wasn't supposed to talk about those matters."

"But he's not here now."

"He's not, but that's not the only thing. Gaspard has purposefully tried to keep me away from you over the past week and a half, so that we couldn't speak again."

"What makes you think that?"

"It's not a thought. I heard him confess that to his wife yesterday morning."

Roger gave his words some thought before uttering, "Something important must've happened then for you to come to me like this."

"Not really. Things haven't changed here much in the past five years, no matter how much Gaspard keeps saying the opposite," Nsala explained. "I've been here for that whole time, and I feel that you're the first outsider who wants to actually do something for us."

"There have been others before me, missionaries and journalists, for example. It was their initiative that led me to come here."

"I don't know about that. I've never met anyone like you. At first, I was hesitant of you, too, thinking that you were just another passer-by. One of the people who look around a bit, shake hands with Gaspard, and then leave just as soon as they arrived. It took me some time to realize that you were different, how you gave water to those men tied to the poles, and explained to me things about Europe that I didn't know," Nsala recalled. "But you'll leave soon, and I fear that if I don't show this place to you now, then it's a chance that I'll never get again."

"Lucas is a good man as well, is he not? Have you shown this place to him?"

"He already knows of everything, but has chosen to hold his tongue," Nsala said silently. "Sometimes he speaks of Christ to defend his silence, sometimes of Leopold, but to me the two feel like the same thing. Something that he fears, and makes him stay his hand."

They passed by someone. A lone, wilted figure appeared from the dark and sauntered forward. It gave them a passing look before its eyes returned to the mud. Somehow it knew where to step in the darkness to go where it needed to. The only sounds in that passing moment were the splashing mud and raindrops that kept pounding on Roger's umbrella. One of them angered the lone flame at his fingertips.

"There's so much suffering in Congo that I find it difficult to believe that someone who has spent time here would keep quiet about it," Roger said when the figure had disappeared back into the darkness. "I trust Lucas on what he has told me about not agreeing with Gaspard, but his words haven't done any good."

"No, they haven't done any good for any of us."

"Do you then think that Lucas has simply grown indifferent to everything that he has seen? That nowadays he can't bring himself to care anymore?"

"I don't know. Maybe. All I know is that people like Gaspard and Lucas have kept things about this place from you," Nsala said and pointed towards the nothingness around them. "The destruction I told you about was much more thorough. These lands were once farmyards and grazing lands for animals, and for children to play on. The Belgians burned down all of it to make room for their plantations. And they're still not done."

"Then with all of this, how do you know your own village is still there?"

Nsala fell silent for a moment, like he always did before speaking of more personal matters. Then he uttered, "You asked me about my daughter before."

"I did. You didn't want to talk about her."

"No."

"If you still don't want to, we don't have to."

"No, I...I want to talk about her. I want to talk about her this time," Nsala reassured himself. "The reason why any of us work here is that the Belgians have our families, our wives, children and parents, as hostages. If we wouldn't work, then we'd risk losing our families. This place that I want to show to you, the place I wanted to tell you about before but didn't, it has to do with that. My daughter. The certainty that she's still alive. The certainty that I haven't spent the last five years on this earth for nothing."

"Nsala, if you're not absolutely certain about this, we don't..."

"I've never been more certain of anything in my life," Nsala spoke over him. "It's a dark place, but an important one. A place you must see before leaving tomorrow."

"Alright then," Roger said and loosened his shoulders. "Alright."

The woods around Bomenga very heavy. The trees hung heavy from the day's torrent that had yet to die down. It would've been difficult enough to catch sleep with the raindrops pounding on the houses' straw roofs, so they both fell quiet to not accidentally wake up anyone. The only other lights in the dark were a few dim squares that shone past closed reed curtains of the houses lining the muddy main street.

Nsala led Roger towards a large wooden house, the same house that served as the village's house of communion. A light flickered from an open window. It led to a room at the back of the house where Nsala had stood some two weeks ago.

His steps became slower and his shoulders stood up more the closer they crept. It was like he expected something bad to happen. If it had occurred to him that stalking around in a pitch black night with an unaware white man holding an oil lamp was a bad idea, it was too late for that now. A shadow stood up and blocked out some of the light coming from the window.

"Alphonse?" a voice called out. "Alphonse, is that you?"

"Father?" Nsala answered with a slight tremble in his voice. "It's you, my child."

The crouched figure made its way down the porch and into the light.

"I'm so glad to see you. I've been wanting to see you, but what are you doing here at this time?" Lucas proclaimed. He would've taken hold of Nsala's shoulders as well had he not backed away.

"What's wrong, Alphonse?"

"If…if you've wanted to come to see me, why haven't you?" Nsala stammered.

"I've wanted to, but there hasn't been an opportunity for that. You've either been tied to helping Gaspard at the mansion, or I've been too busy helping Mr Casement with his work around the lake. I've been wanting to ask you how you've settled in with Gaspard and Cécile."

"Good enough, I guess."

"Gaspard hasn't given you too much work, I trust?"

"More than what you did, but not more than what I had before."

"That's good to hear. And I trust that in my absence Mr Casement has made Gaspard behave properly?" Lucas asked with a nervous laugh and turned to Roger. "And speaking of you, I thought you left earlier today. What are you still doing here?"

"I had to postpone my departure because of the weather, I'm afraid."

"Well, it has indeed been a terrible day of rain. But what are you two doing out here then? You'll only catch a flu in this rain."

"There's something that I want to show to Roger before he leaves."

"What exactly do you mean?"

Nsala swallowed hard and looked down. His voice took on a more trembling tone as he spoke between the nods, "You know what I mean. Roger wants to help, and I know that you do too. Therefore I want to show Roger the grave."

"A grave? What grave do you mean? The graveyard behind the church?"

"The other one."

"What other one?" Lucas asked. "There has only ever been the graveyard behind the church."

"You know very well what I mean."

"My child, do you have a particular loved one buried in the graveyard that I haven't heard of? Is that what you wish to show Mr Casement before he leaves us?"

"Father, you don't need to come with us if you don't want any part in it. Just let us pass so that I can show Roger what I want him to see. There's no harm in it."

Lucas didn't say a word after that, but it was clear that hesitation had taken over him. Nsala sighed from frustration and waved at Roger to follow him. He took a step forward, but Lucas placed his hand over Nsala's chest to stop him there. He didn't resist.

"My child, there are things in this world that are not meant for us to understand," Lucas said in a quiet voice.

"Are you still trying to deny everything that has happened here? To fool yourself into thinking that what we've seen is something that we can't do anything about?"

"It's simply better for you two to leave."

"What does it take to make you understand, father?"

"Alphonse, please…"

"How much more it takes until you finally feel compelled to do the same as Roger has done? How many more punishments? How many more burned down villages?" Nsala barked and pushed Lucas' arm aside. In the moment's anger, he spooled his shirt around his right fist, turned around and asked one final question, "How many more lashings will it take?"

The feeble light at Roger's fingertips revealed a patchwork of fresh, reddish scars running across his back. The blood on most of them had only recently dried up.

"My child, who did this to you?"

"Someone who works for the person you're still defending."

"Was it David?" Roger asked.

Nsala nodded over his shoulder.

"David?" Lucas repeated. "Why would he do something like that? What did you do to provoke him?"

"Nothing! I did absolutely nothing. He came to see me after Henrik's burial. He blamed me for having to bury him, and said they had been friends," Nsala told. "I don't know if what he said was true or not, but the scars he gave me are real enough."

"Please, for the sake of decency, but your shirt back on," Lucas said with a shiver. "Why did you show those horrible things to us?"

"I didn't want to," Nsala said and pulled the shirt back on with some effort. "I'd hoped to avoid meeting you altogether. But I need to show the grave to Roger, and I need to know that you'll let us through."

"What David did to you is horrible. It's exactly what I've asked Gaspard to look into."

"Only he has yet to do anything about these things," Roger stepped in.

"At least, he hasn't killed anyone."

"You've said that same, lame excuse before."

"Good intentions are all he has to offer at this stage, I'm afraid. The Free State is barely eighteen years old, and development has been slow, especially…"

"This far from the coast," Roger finished his sentence. "Yes, I know the sermon by now. You said it yourself that there's nothing more to be gained from Gaspard. So why even bother reasoning with him if he won't listen to you, never mind defending him?"

"I…I think you're right," Lucas said between heavy breaths. His head flopped down and he leaned in on his cane while he croaked, "You're right. There's no point in defending a man like him. And there's something I need to confess to you. I've been lying to you this whole time."

"After everyone else has done it as well, I'm not sure I should be surprised."

"I'm not proud of it."

"Then why did you lie?"

"Because…because Gaspard asked me to do it. He asked me to lie to you if necessary. He knew I'd done it before to other visitors, and that nobody would expect a sad, crippled man like me to side with the oppressor."

"What are the things you lied to me about exactly?"

"The two locals you met here in Bomenga that had lost their hands…well, they had only lost them recently."

"It's true," Nsala said. "I left that out."

"You left it out?" Roger asked and turned to Nsala.

"I did."

"Why?"

"I guess…I guess we were both afraid."

"Afraid?" Roger asked. "Afraid of whom?"

"Of you."

"Me?"

"Yes. It's like I told you on our way here. How could any of us have been sure that you weren't just another agent sent here by the state to write a rosy report to hide the truth?"

"There's a very real fear of reporting these things to the authorities. And it's not only the locals who are affected by it," Lucas said. "I've felt shocked over the things I've seen here, but I haven't been able to overcome that same fear the way Alphonse has."

"Is there something else that I've been lied to about?"

"I lied to you during our visits to all of those villages around the lake," Lucas admitted. "For example, the chief we met at the last village told me that all of his young wives had been given to him from a nearby village that had been recently burned down. It had been a gift from the white devil, but also a reminder of what happened to those who turned against him."

"The village must've been Julienne's," Nsala added. "During my second night at the mansion, the same when Gaspard had you over for dinner, Julienne told me that her village was visited by some soldiers. People were killed at random. The surviving men were taken here, the rest forced into labour, and livestock taken."

"So you're saying to me that the roasted lamb was served to me at a gunpoint?" Roger put the pieces of the puzzle together. Nsala gave him a shy nod as an answer, and Roger breathed in deep.

"After Henrik's burial, I urged you to leave Bikoro as soon as possible," Lucas continued. "I wanted you to leave as soon as possible so that things would've seemed more harmless in your report than they are."

"And you would've succeeded if Nsala hadn't come to me."

"I owe the church my life for guiding me away from the cramped slums of Charleroi where violence and poverty were the norm. Bomenga has been no different from home," Lucas explained. "I think that past made it so easy for me to become jaded to everything I've seen here, and the church's views are the same as the fatherland's."

"That of Leopold's?"

"Yes. I only hoped that my work in teaching the locals French and God's word would help them lead better lives, perhaps not in this life, but in the next," Lucas said and looked at Nsala. He forced a shy smile over his lips, "I guess, in some small ways, it did."

"It might've actually been all the difference," Nsala said. "Otherwise I wouldn't have been able to tell Roger any of this."

Lucas turned his good eye to Roger and said, "Maybe. All I know is that ultimately it wasn't me who helped you in your work. And now I only feel shame for it."

"It takes a strong man to deny what's right in front of him. And if the truth becomes unbearable, you create your own," Roger said.

Lucas gave his words a silent nod before his head sunk back down. Nsala placed his hand over his shoulder and said, "I've learned enough of Christ from you to know that he's merciful, and I know you well enough to see that staying silent on what you've seen has only brought you pain over the years. There's still time to make amends by choosing to do the right thing now."

"What could I possibly do but continue to suffer in silence?"

"If you choose that route, all that pain will only get stronger with time. You'll suffer from it for the rest of your life. You'll wake up at nights with shock, find yourself covered in sweat, year after year, until you meet your god's grace."

"So you never believed in Him?" Lucas muttered. "I shouldn't hold you at fault for that. I haven't shown the best example."

"Father, you're not the only one struggling with the pain of regret," Nsala said. "I regret that I didn't stand up for my daughter the only time I had a chance to do that. I haven't been given another opportunity to make things right for her, and that thought still haunts me."

"You've told me."

"I know you don't agree with Gaspard. You've never agreed, and here's your chance to finally make things right. It's a chance I haven't been afforded. So I only ask that you'd let me show the grave to Roger."

"Yes. Yes, you're right, Alphonse. And I can do better than that. I know the grave you mean, my child," Lucas said with a sudden sharpness that took hold of him. "Please, let me lead you to it."

"I know all too well where it is."

"Then please, let me come with you. I also need to see it again. To face again what I've tried to forget."

Nsala gave Roger an uneasy look. Just recently he had attempted to prevent the two from going forward, but now was asking to come along. Was it that easy for a man to change and let go of the beliefs they had harboured for years? Or was it so easy for the reason that he had just dropped a burden off of his shoulders that had weighed him down for years?

"If you want, then please, lead on," Roger said to Lucas. "I have no idea what we're looking for. The more there are of us, the easier it will be to find."

His plea seemed genuine, and the show of trust made Lucas let out a long breath. It left a hanging whiff in the cold air before it disappeared beyond the moving light's reach.

The two led Roger to the edge of a dark forest dripping with steam. Out here, by the border of the dark canopy, the smell of decaying plants and wood that Roger had become so accustomed to in the past months grew stronger.

"Is this the place?" he asked. "This is the place," Lucas said.

Nsala kneeled down and slid his hand over the mud. He took some of it in his hand and inspected it close to his face before tilting his hand slightly to the side. The wet mud slid down his palm.

"This is the place," Nsala repeated and stood back up. "I remember this place. I would never forget it."

The place was only a stone's toss away from the low wooden fence that ran around the graveyard behind the church. It was there that haphazardly erected crosses marked some hundred or so graves. Maybe it was just Roger's imagination, as it was impossible to tell such things after a heavy rain, but the ground here looked recently disturbed. Whatever the truth was, the bulldog John picked up a scent and pointed its snout towards a spot in the mud. It scraped at the spot with its front paw.

"Your dog must've smelt something," Lucas said. "I only remembered now that we should've taken a pair of shovels with us."

"There's no need for that," Nsala said. He kneeled back down and dug his bare hands deep into the mud. John stepped back and looked Roger in the eyes. The look was enough to convince Roger to fold his umbrella, give the oil lamp to Lucas and to sink his hands in as well. The cold, wet mud felt hideous. Lucas stood behind them, leaning onto his cane and holding out the light.

For a while, their hands shovelled the mud away. At first, it felt almost pointless. He still didn't know what they were even looking for, or how deep they'd have to dig. So far all that he had gotten out of the night was mud in his clothes and a compulsive feeling to clean under his fingernails. But some unseen force, a desire to find out what it was that had brought them here and convinced Lucas to join their quest for justice, was enough to help him keep going and find out.

Then he felt something odd. Something solid that still gave in a bit. His expression caught Nsala's attention, and they removed the earth around the object together. What they found was a lone, leathery hand peeking out of the mud.

Nsala shuddered at the realization of what it was, but then said, "No, this...this is not it."

"It's not what?" Roger asked.

"Not what I was looking for. There must be more."

"More hands like this? Nsala, what are you saying?"

"Those who die from exhaustion, hunger, or disease are buried in the church's backyard," Lucas said. "Sometimes, however, people die from loss of blood after their hands have been cut off."

"Have been cut off..." Roger repeated. "Are you saying that...?"

"I'm afraid so. This place is where those hands are buried."

Nsala dug up a piece of another arm. This one was only bone. He placed it to the side and threw his arms back into the mud. Soon he unearthed another, one that was more recent, still rotting and a home to a colony of maggots. He grew more desperate with each arm that he dug up until he finally found what he was looking for: a hand that was smaller than all the others.

He collapsed at the sight of it and barely caught himself with his elbows. His entire body shook before he let out a muffled cry.

The realization of it all swept over Roger. He passed his eyes over the hands peeking out from the mud. He breathed fast. Then he asked, "When you spoke of that certainty that your daughter was still alive, did you...did you mean...this?"

Nsala gave a shaking nod to the ground. He was only barely holding back the tears and anguish that had been locked away all this time.

"This was the place where I got to hold my daughter's hand for the last time," he stuttered at last before his voice broke down into a dry croak. He bit his lips together, and after a moment breathed in deep. He almost whispered, "The last time I saw her was when they cut off her hand. Then the Belgians took her away, and had me throw the hand here while holding a barrel of a gun on my head."

"My goodness…why did any of that happen?"

"There was half a litre of rubber missing from my bucket. It was all the reason they needed. It all happened some months ago, not long after the rainy season began."

"That's at least five months," Roger counted.

"Maybe. I don't know. I don't care," Nsala said. "All I know is that I haven't seen my daughter since then, and I'm afraid. I've been so afraid for her this whole time. There's only the two of us in this world. She's the only reason that has kept me going through all of these years, and if she's gone I…I…"

"I can't even begin to imagine your fear, or if your own daughter feels the same."

"What if she thinks I lost my hand as well? Or that I'm dead, and she's an orphan? They are fears that I can't do anything about," Nsala said. Tears ran down his cheeks, and the skin around his eyes had turned into wrinkles.

"Nsala, showing this place to me was the right thing to do," Roger assured him. "I had no idea that this kind of brutality had still taken place around here, and I would've never known if you hadn't shown it to me."

"I've only known of this place, but never actually stood here so close to it," Lucas said. "Seeing it all now, like this, I understand those feelings that you've struggled with. I should've listened to you about them."

"Will you...will you make sure that people will learn about this place?" Nsala asked. His eyes drifted between the two.

Roger closed his eyes and gave him a slow nod.

"Will you make sure that no one will ever again have to go through what my daughter went through? What I've gone through?"

"Nsala, you have my word on that. As soon as I get back to Boma, I'll make sure that everyone will learn about these things that you've told and shown me."

Nsala looked back at the ground, at the small leathery hand sitting in a mud pit. His eyes stayed there for a moment. Then he reluctantly pushed mud over the hand, ready to bury the same thing that had given him so much pain and worry just now.

Soon all the hands were buried in the ground once again. The victims would do nothing with the remains. Better to let them rest now before the world would know of them. The drizzle would make sure that by morning it'd look like no one had ever visited the place.

This unwanted graveyard must've been in use for years, long before Nsala, Lucas or even Gaspard had come to know of its existence. Each hand had belonged to a different person. Who knew how many more of them were hidden under the damp soil.

Roger didn't want to know the precise numbers. He didn't need to know. All he needed was a small piece of the whole, and the knowledge that the place had gone unseen for a long time, right next to the church's graveyard. The only difference between the two was that the former's graves were unmarked, unwished for. Unwanted.

13. Clipped Wings

"You can still see the smokestack of the steamer that my wife's on," Gaspard said and squinted at the distance under a cupped palm. "Ungrateful swine."

Roger returned him an inquisitive look but said nothing.

"I gave Cécile everything to make her happy here, but it wasn't enough for her. I gave her a roof over her head, made sure she didn't have to go hungry, and even put up with her horrible paintings. Was it my fault that she didn't fulfil her part of the marriage?"

"Well, I've never been married myself, so I can't say anything on that."

"No, you wouldn't, but I think you'll have a lot more to say on Congo," Gaspard remarked with a lack of enthusiasm. "I think this is the last time we'll see each other, and then you'll be gone forever like my wife."

"I intend to get back to the coast sooner than later."

"That, actually, reminds me that I never received any mail or document that would give the governor-general's blessing for your work here."

"It must still be on its way. You said it yourself that there isn't much of a postal infrastructure in Congo to speak of."

"Hmm, lost in mail. But of course. That must be it," Gaspard remarked. "In any case, I don't think I ever asked you why you came to Congo in particular."

"I think we have touched that subject several times already."

"Well yes, but just why is there such an international ruckus about Congo? What has made this particular place a centrepiece of all that hate and condemnation that led to you coming here?"

Roger was about to open his mouth when Gaspard continued, "I've heard and read similar reports of abuse from elsewhere in Africa, from colonies owned by Germany and Portugal for example. And what about the rest of the world then? The Native Americans, the Chinese, and all the Indians and Aboriginals in colonies ruled by the same British Empire that you serve. Why does nobody care about them? What is it about Congo that makes the entire Europe care so much about this place in particular, but not lift even a finger for the rest?"

"The main difference, to my observations, is that Congo is King Leopold's personal colony," Roger noted. "You must've noticed it as well, but almost all of the public anger and accusations have been directed at Leopold rather than the Free State."

"Yes. And why do you think it's so?"

"It's far easier to hate one man than it is to hate an entire nation."

"Exactly, good consul. You've found the root of the problem," Gaspard said. "People are hypocrites and always act on their emotions first and foremost. Just like my wife. This is the reason why all the lies aimed at my king have grown out of control. Congo is no different from the rest of the world. We might've had our differences, but I sincerely hope that your work will prove His Excellency's innocence."

Gaspard turned around without waiting for a response. Yesterday's torrent was only a bad memory reflected in the pools of water his boots stomped on. Nsala and Julienne had been there behind them the whole time. The latter gave Roger a quick glance over her shoulder before turning around and following on Gaspard's heels. It was impossible to tell if her eyes hid in them distress or simply confusion that he was leaving all of a sudden.

Nsala, however, stayed behind. He waited for Gaspard to walk out of earshot before taking a step forward and extending his hand.

"What's this?" Roger asked.

"A handshake. Isn't this how you Europeans say goodbye to friends?"

"A goodbye, among other things," Roger said and took hold of Nsala's hand. He had a strong grip despite his hand's sleek form.

"Do you think your work will help give peace to all the families in Congo?" Nsala asked before he released his hold.

"Yes. After what you showed me last night, I'm sure it will. Leopold can't get away with what he's done in Congo much longer. No one should go through what you and your daughter have gone through."

"I hope it'll be so. And I hope we'll see each other again under better circumstances. I'd like to show you to my village, and for you to meet my daughter."

"You know, it can take several months before my report makes it to Europe," Roger said before Nsala got too far. "And from there, it might take years for anything to happen in Congo."

"Don't worry about me," Nsala said, and tried to force a smile on his cracked lips. "I'll take care of myself. Yesterday was painful, but it reminded me why I've been fighting for so long."

Gaspard had only now noticed his favourite servant's absence, and hollered at him from the mansion's doorstep. Roger and Nsala exchanged quick, final nods before walking the opposite ways. Soon the small steamer left port, chasing after the fleeing smokestack to the west.

* * *

The rainy season turned to the dry season, and then back to the rainy season again. The only permanent change they brought with them was a pile of newspapers and letters in Gaspard's office that, which each passing month, grew taller as more and more of the correspondence was left unread until the ones at the bottom of the pile began to take on a light yellow tone from all the moisture that kept seeping in.

Most of the correspondence was in French, but some in other languages. Few of them reminded Nsala of the familiar European tongue, and the others not so much. What had begun as innocent curiosity by skimming through the headlines soon turned into a habit of loitering around for a while after picking up the triweekly mail delivery. Sometimes he didn't even need to read the news to guess what the people in the faraway land were talking about, as he was greeted by a black and white photo of a familiar, bearded man.

Casement had returned to Britain and turned in his report to the parliament, just like he said he would. What followed had been a continent-wide uproar for justice, only to be met by a chorus of voices ready to stand against it. Sometimes the news were about other Europeans who had witnessed the same cruelties as Roger had in Congo, and now added their experiences to the horror story that kept taking shape. But just as often the news were about Europeans who had witnessed none of the atrocities, and instead hailed Congo's monarch as a paragon of everything that the Western civilization stood for.

The tug of war seemed to go on forever. Other news began to take their place alongside Casement's report: a war in a land called Manchuria between two empires fighting over the carcass of a third, the beginning of a continent-splitting construction work somewhere in Panama, the death of the hero Stanley who had handed Congo to the hated Leopold on a silver platter, and the slaughter of Africans by German bayonets somewhere south of Congo. Ultimately it felt like Casement had never even been to Congo.

It was around those times that Nsala stopped reading the news. Gaspard hadn't been the same since Cécile had left him, no matter how strained their relationship had been from the start. He rarely left the mansion anymore, and neither did Julienne. The day to day affairs of managing the trading post and its wilting plantations were left to Lucas and David. To help the former with his new-found duties, Gaspard let Nsala go and return to Bomenga.

* * *

"No, it's not quite like that," Nsala said and tapped on a book's page. "When speaking of past events in the simple tense, you need to pronounce the letter e at the end of the verb, if it has one. Let me come up with an example."

He pronounced a simple sentence, and then allowed the others to try and repeat it. For a moment, the church's front yard was filled with dozens of voices repeating the same short phrase to varying levels of success.

"That's closer to it, good. But remember that some verbs have irregular forms," Nsala commented. "They're something you simply must learn by heart."

"I don't really know, Nsala. What's even the point of learning French anymore?" someone brought up in Bangi.

"I agree," another man voiced. "We've been learning French for years now, and never used it for anything."

"You never know when you might need French. If you had known it when Roger was here, you would've been able to tell him your stories as well."

"Maybe, but what good did it do to you? He's been gone for a long time now, and hasn't returned. And no one else has come here since then."

"Lucas speaks good Bangi, doesn't he? He's the one giving us the news and tasks. What's the point of making a hundred people learn a new language when the only person that matters has already learned ours?"

"I think you should listen to what your students have to say," a voice announced in French. Nsala turned around to see a tall person standing behind him.

"David."

"What was that?"

"I mean, Officer Fidèle."

David returned him a self-indulgent hum. He placed his foot down on a rock and leaned in his elbow against his knee.

"I thought that teaching French was Lucas' job," he said after a while.

"He wasn't feeling so good today, and allowed me to hold the class today."

"Is that so?" David said and tossed the book out of his hands. "There's no point for you or the others to learn French. You'll never use it for anything, anyway."

The book landed at the foot of one student sitting on the ground. He backed away a bit. Others around him did the same after him out of instinct, but Nsala stayed where he was.

"Or, I almost forgot, there was that one thing you used French for," David said and looked down on Nsala. "You fed lies to the British consul. It's because of you that things have gone downhill since his visit."

"What are you saying?"

"You can't be blind to your own actions. Gaspard rarely leaves the mansion anymore because dealing with all those lies in the newspapers and letters takes up all his time. At the same time, you fiddle around teaching French to the others instead of working in the fields. You have a duty to your king, to your country, and Gaspard doesn't have the time to see to it that you do it because of the mess you helped to create."

"Name something, anything that I told him."

"He specifically asked to work with you. I was the one who brought you to him, remember? And later I saw you two talk."

"You have to be more specific than that."

"I don't need to know what you whispered into his ear to know that things haven't been the same since his visit."

"You believe in the Belgians and their values, don't you, Officer *Fidèle*," Nsala said and stood up. "What does the 'innocence until proven guilty' mean to you?"

"Watch your tone."

"You have no proof for your accusations. What you're saying is just…"

David grasped his outstretched arm and yanked down. The movement forced Nsala down on his knees. His arm got slammed over the tree stump he had used as a stool.

"I've had it with you and your insubordination," David yelled and reached for something with his free hand. Nsala bit his teeth together. He managed to look up to see the blade of a large knife being unsheathed from its scabbard before the pain from the fingernails biting into his wrist forced his head down.

"There's only one way this will end. We'll see if you feel brave after this."

"What in the name of God is happening here?" Nsala heard a frail voice ask.

"This doesn't concern you, old man," David glanced at approaching Lucas. "Back off!"

"But, that's Alphonse you have there," Lucas said and looked at the elevated blade. "What has he done wrong?"

"I said back off!"

"Gaspard would never allow you to do something like that without a reason."

"Roger and his little rat got into your head too, didn't they?" David said and turned his attention back to Nsala. "Gaspard won't miss him at all."

The blade fell down and a shriek filled the air. It hadn't been enough to cut through the bone, and David had to yank the blade free with some effort in front of the horrified onlookers. The struggling only made the screams worse before a second slash separated the arm from its stump.

"What are you crying? Have you forgotten that you begged for me to take both of your hands instead of your daughter's hand?" David mocked, let go of the stump and tossed the loose hand away without looking at it. "Only one more and you've received your wish."

"David, you've gone too far! This isn't right."

"Gaspard is too busy to deal with what happens outside of his mansion," David proclaimed and pointed the bloodied knife at Lucas. "That's why he put me and you in charge of this place. And between us two, you're nothing but a cripple."

David took a step towards Lucas. He tapped the ground with his cane a few times, as if searching for support, and mumbled something. He didn't get to finish before David pushed him with his free hand. Lucas stumbled, dropped his cane and after a few seconds of flailing his arms around he fell over on his back.

"This doesn't concern you, cripple. Just leave," David said and returned to Nsala. He kept shuddering and could only look at what remained of his right hand in a pool of bright blood. He didn't resist when David reached for his other hand.

"You sold your own kin to the white devils!"

David dropped the hand. His eyes darted to the crowd around him. It had grown in size as more had flocked to see what was going on.

"Who said that?" David demanded and pointed the blade forward. "Who said that?"

"You're just a tool for the Belgians," another voice called out.

David turned to the left and picked someone seemingly at random, "It was you, wasn't it? I'll have your hand for that as well."

He took hurried steps forward and the others backed away. Several new voices called out from the crowd.

"Traitor!"

"Liar!"

"Brute!"

The voices grew more frequent and bolder. David stopped in his tracks. He breathed deep, turning in place, his eyes darting from one mocking mouth to another. Then a stone hit him in the back of his head. He reeled forward but caught his balance and turned around with the blade pointed forward.

"I'll have all of your hands for this! All of them! Then we'll see how easy it will be for you to feed your children and parents."

Someone jumped on David from behind and pulled his arms around his throat. The blade fell down as his hands clawed at the arms. He collapsed down with an angry croak and disappeared in the middle of a seething crowd.

Nsala watched on between laboured breaths. He wished to feel happy at the sight of a crowd mauling a man to death, someone he hated, but he felt nothing. No sense of justice or redemption that should've been there. The only thing he wanted to do was to cry from pain, but he couldn't bring himself to do so. He needed to do that somewhere alone, far away from everyone else. He wanted to stand up, but was afraid his legs would give out if he tried to do so.

"Alphonse," he heard a familiar, low voice say over the clamour. "Nsala...Thank God you're still here. Quick, we need to get that hand tended to."

* * *

The stacks of newspapers didn't stop arriving despite that they went unread by their intended recipient. The criticism towards Leopold never truly died down, only shifted up and down, and eventually it was enough. The façade that he had worked so tirelessly to build for decades and then maintain was torn down.

In late autumn, a little over five years since Roger and Nsala had shaken hands by the pier, Gaspard left for Boma to toast the Belgian government that took over Congo from the Free State and its old monarch. Gaspard returned with empty hands and sloughed back inside the lonely mansion, while the people outside still had their obligations.

It took more time, some years still, before a letter came one day. Unlike so many others, it didn't go unread. A skeleton crawled out of the mansion to announce the news.

It all happened without fanfare. First, there was confusion among the locals, disbelief. With sufficient time, a realization set in: they were free, all of them. Their freedom had been decreed by old men in a distant land none of them had ever set foot in. A land built tall by riches taken from Congo in blood and sweat.

The men departed from the plantations to all directions. Some who had lost everyone and everything else in the long years opted to stay, now able to live life as they wished. But Nsala wasn't among them. He accompanied a small number of other men on their way back home, to a place they hadn't seen in almost fifteen years despite that the journey took only a week by foot. On the way back, the only thing in his mind was his daughter. How much she must've grown, how much must've happened in her life in his absence. She was a woman by now!

Someone announced the group of shambling corpses approaching the village. The initial confusion and fear soon turned to joy as gaunt women and adolescents rushed to meet the living dead by the village's edge. In the hassle, everyone tried to find their loved ones. Husbands and wives who hadn't felt each other's touch in an eternity, men who could barely identify their little children after so much time, and elderly who had forgotten what their sons' faces had looked like.

The one person Nsala was looking for wasn't in the crowd. Some were only now clambering out of their homes to see the unexpected celebration outside and making their way to join in. Nsala left the others and headed towards the place where he remembered his home to be.

The air became quieter the further away he walked. Someone, a young woman, ran past him, and gave him a passing glance. She wasn't her.

Birdsong replaced the murmurs in the distance. Nsala found his home where he remembered it to be, but the yard was empty, and no one answered when he announced his return in a low voice.

He stepped past the weathered cloth covering the doorway. He called for his daughter by her name, Oleka, but heard no answer. He made his way to the back of the single room, and pulled back the cloth covering the doorway to the backyard.

He collapsed down on his knees. He yanked his remaining hand to cover his mouth, but it was too heavy and fell down.

There was a grave. A small, unremarkable grave. The air stood still apart from a cry that turned into a sob. There was no rain to wash away the tears this time.

Printed in the USA
CPSIA information can be obtained
at www.ICGtesting.com
LVHW011430260923
759277LV00008B/155